Ken Ludwig's Moriarty

A New Sherlock Holmes Adventure

SAMUEL FRENCH

MUSIC AND THIRD-PARTY MATERIALS USE NOTE

IMPORTANT BILLING AND CREDIT REQUIREMENTS

KEN LUDWIG'S MORIARTY was first produced by the Cleveland Play House (Mark Cuddy, Guest Artistic & Managing Director), Cleveland, OH, and premiered on April 29, 2023. The performance was directed by Mark Brokaw and Michael Barakiva, with scenic design by Chika Shimizu, costume design by Lex Liang, lighting design by David Lander, and original music and sound design by Lindsay Jones. The Production Stage Manager was John Godbout. The cast was as follows:

SHERLOCK HOLMES . . . . .Christian Pedersen

DOCTOR WATSON . . . . Nick Gaswirth

MORIARTY, KING OTTO, & OTHERS . . . . Jeffrey M. Bender

IRENE ADLER, MRS. HUDSON, & CARTWRIGHT . . . . . . Olivia Gilliatt

DAISY, MRS. BARABAS, HILDA KLEBB, & OTHERS. . . . . . . .Talley Gale

CHARACTERS

The play is written for five actors

Actor One
>SHERLOCK HOLMES

Actor Two
>DOCTOR WATSON

Actor Three
>RUPERT PERKINS
>KING OTTO VON ORMSTEIN
>PROFESSOR MORIARTY
>MRS. GASNER
>PORTER
>CONDUCTOR
>PADDY KEYS
>NEFERTITI
>MYCROFT HOLMES
>LESTRADE
>ROUGH WITH A BLUDGEON
>BARTENDER
>ANNOUNCER

Actor Four
>IRENE ADLER
>MRS. HUDSON
>CARTWRIGHT

Actor Five
>MIROSLAV HAČEK
>DAISY
>MILKER
>VICAR
>MRS. BARABAS
>HILDA KLEBB
>TOBY
>CAB DRIVER
>HANS

SETTING

The action of the play takes place in London,
Cambridgeshire, and Europe

TIME

Circa 1891

AUTHOR'S NOTE

I did not intend to become an author of Sherlock Holmes plays. Then again, Arthur Conan Doyle didn't intend to become known for writing Sherlock Holmes adventures either. But the character he created is such an iconic force of nature that he's hard to resist.

In 2015, I premiered a theatrical adaptation of the most famous and oft-read Sherlock Holmes adventure, *The Hound of the Baskervilles*. Entitled *Baskerville*, the play was a one-off: a straightforward adaptation of one of the greatest adventure novels ever written. When I conceived it, I gave myself an extra challenge by writing it for only five actors, thereby hoping to make the play as much about the world of the theatre as it was about Sherlock Holmes. In the end, this device – using five actors to play over thirty-five characters – gave the piece an antic theatricality that I liked.

Selecting *The Hound of the Baskervilles* as the underlying story for a play about Sherlock Holmes proved to be a good decision for several reasons. *The Hound of the Baskervilles* is a novella – a short novel – and therefore the perfect length for a play. It has a terrific villain in the oddball butterfly hunter, Jack Stapleton; an endearing romance between young lovers; and two main locales of romantic proportions: fog-shrouded Victorian London, and the vast mysterious beauty of the Devonshire moorlands. Throw in a gothic manor house, an escaped convict, and a glowing hell-hound, and you have the perfect recipe for a mystery play.

Baskerville proved to be a success on stage, so I decided to return to Holmes and Watson to see if they had another stage adventure in them. And if I had another in me.

When I decided to write a second Sherlock Holmes adventure for the stage, I found a much harder task ahead of me. Conan Doyle wrote three other Holmes novellas, *A Study in Scarlet*, *The Sign of the Four*, and *The Valley of Fear*, but I found their stories too byzantine for a good play, and none has the wonderful pulse of *The Hound of the Baskervilles*. I then turned to the fifty-six short stories that Conan Doyle wrote about

Holmes and Watson, and while I found endless examples of Conan Doyle's trademark crisp character portraits and well-built mysteries, even the best of them, including perennial favorites like "Silver Blaze," "The Blue Carbuncle," and "The Speckled Band," were too short for a complete play. With no single novella or short story to rely on, I needed a different approach to this piece, and I made two decisions early in the process that shaped the play at every stage.

First, I decided to change the genre. *Baskerville* is a comedy-mystery – a classic whodunnit, as are most of the Sherlock Holmes stories and novellas. In a classic whodunnit, the heart of the narrative is the mystery, with its string of suspects, clues, and deductions. As I cast about for a plot for my new play, I read "The Final Problem" several times, always asking myself why this story in particular was so compelling to me. It is the one and only Sherlock Holmes story in which Professor Moriarty appears, which is notable in itself, considering the long afterlife Holmes's nemesis has had in pastiches and adaptations. Beyond that, though, I decided that what's truly unusual about "The Final Problem" is that it's not a mystery at all. It's a melodrama.

A melodrama is essentially a popular work of fiction, often for the stage, filled with sensationalized moments of danger, agony, and fear, peopled with exaggerated characters, and primarily intended to appeal to the emotions. Melodramas depend heavily on plot as opposed to complex moral issues. And the characters are often stereotyped into heroes, heroines, helpmeets, and villains.

Historically, hundreds of melodramas were written for the stage in the nineteenth and early twentieth centuries. My own favorite is *Tosca*, both the play by Sardou and the opera by Puccini. The opera is now one of the most popular musical works of all time, but when it first appeared, it was referred to as "that shabby little shocker." Another favorite is *Ruddigore*, the operetta by Gilbert and Sullivan, which is a satire of melodrama. I also have a particular fondness for *The Bells*, one of the greatest triumphs of the most famous British actor of the second half of the nineteenth century, Sir Henry Irving. Indeed, *The Bells* was so popular in its day that Irving programmed the play at the Lyceum Theatre year after year, always playing the starring role.

The form also offers opportunities for spectacular set pieces. One of these came ready to order in "The Final Problem": the final, fatal struggle at the Reichenbach Falls between Sherlock Holmes and Professor Moriarty. As described by Watson, the Reichenbach Falls is

> a fearful place. The torrent, swollen by the melting snow, plunges into a tremendous abyss, from which the spray rolls up like the smoke from a burning house. The shaft into which the river hurls itself is an immense chasm, lined by glistening coal-black rock, and narrowing into a creaming, boiling pit of incalculable depth.

The setting is tailor-made for the emotional grandeur of a melodrama. Luckily for me, creating such an abysm of death on stage is the work of designers; as a playwright, I need only write "Scene Eight: The Reichenbach Falls."

An additional draw of writing a melodrama was the opportunity to create a play full of chases, show-downs, shoot-outs, and other types of derring-do that characterized a half century of our English-language stage tradition. Plays of this kind went out of fashion by the 1920s, at which point drama moved into the world of naturalism. But as I read and reread the fifty-six short stories of the Sherlock Holmes canon in search of a plot for my new play, I decided that the melodramatic form was the sandbox I wanted to play in. It suits the grand world of Sherlock Holmes, and *Moriarty* is my homage to the tradition.

The second decision I made in writing *Moriarty* was to bring to life all of the most iconic characters that Conan Doyle invented in his brilliant creation of the Sherlock Holmes legend. These include Professor Moriarty from "The Final Problem," Irene Adler from "A Scandal in Bohemia," and Sherlock's brother Mycroft from "The Bruce-Partington Plans." I started with Holmes's arch-nemesis, Professor Moriarty, and their famous mortal struggle. Conan Doyle never explained why, of all his foes, Moriarty's defeat was worth Holmes's very life. In truth, Conan Doyle invented Moriarty simply as a mechanism to kill off his most beloved character so the author could focus his attention on his other literary endeavors. I wanted to give Holmes and Moriarty a history that illuminated their relationship.

I created a back story that dates their relationship to Holmes's days as a student at Cambridge University. Moriarty is a professor, so why not make him Holmes's professor – a beloved mentor who betrayed the trust of his young acolyte and escaped into the underworld to wreak havoc on London. Holmes, blaming himself for failing to see the evil in Moriarty, dedicates his life to bringing criminals to justice in an attempt to atone. And when Moriarty resurfaces, he charges himself with tracking the professor down to a final, deadly confrontation. It seemed to me that this storyline had melodrama written all over it.

The second supporting character I drafted into my play was Irene Adler. Holmes meets Adler in "A Scandal in Bohemia," and she never appears again in any of the stories. While it is clear from the very first sentence that Holmes admires her, he very explicitly does *not* fall in love with her:

To Sherlock Holmes she is always *the* woman. I have seldom heard him mention her under any other name. In his eyes she eclipses and predominates the whole of her sex. It was not that he felt any emotion akin to love for Irene Adler. All emotions, and that one particularly, were abhorrent to his cold, precise but admirably balanced mind. He was, I take it, the most perfect reasoning and observing machine that the world has seen, but as a lover he would have placed himself in a false position.

But a melodrama needs a love story, and like many interpreters of the Sherlock Holmes mythos, I decided to make Irene Adler the love of Sherlock's life. In essence, I wanted to balance the play's sensational battle between good and evil with an equally sensational romance, and how could I resist "*the* woman"?

As depicted in "A Scandal in Bohemia," Adler is American; she is mischievous, brazen, and she challenges Holmes at every turn. I tried to retain the Irene Adler of "Scandal," but I expanded her presence and have her join Holmes on his chase to capture Moriarty, driven by her own quest for revenge against the professor. This brings her to the fearsome Reichenbach Falls along with Holmes and Moriarty, where the final, fatal reckoning of the play takes place.

Finally, I decided to include Holmes's elder brother, Mycroft, as a character in the play. He appears in a few of the short stories, where he is depicted as part of the intelligence service in Her Majesty's government – sometimes speculated by fans to be the prototype for the mysterious M in the James Bond universe. Mycroft is said to be smarter than Sherlock, but too lazy to do the kind of legwork necessary to be a detective. He is a founding member of a private members' club for the most "unsocial and unclubbable" men in London, where no one is allowed to speak aloud. I decided that he, too, was custom-built for melodrama; and frankly, he was just too much fun for a comic playwright to resist. Mycroft led me to the short story "The Bruce-Partington Plans," which became the glue that held the two acts of the play together.

The wider world of Sherlock Holmes is peopled with colorful characters by the dozen, characters with whom we love to spend time – not just Holmes, Watson, Professor Moriarty, Irene Adler, and Mycroft Holmes, but also Mrs. Hudson, Inspector Lestrade, and the Baker Street Irregulars. I was determined that *Moriarty* would include them all.

The ragged band of street kids who help Holmes on his adventures, The Baker Street Irregulars, gave their name to one of the most storied literary societies in the world. The founder of that society – of which I am proud to be a member – called the Sherlock Holmes adventures "a textbook of friendship," and this play centers primarily on the bone-deep friendship of Sherlock Holmes and Dr. Watson. That is the heart of the myth that Conan Doyle created, and *Moriarty* is my attempt to give us all yet another opportunity to experience the comic joy and melodramatic pyrotechnics of the Sherlock Holmes legend. I hope you enjoy this modest addition.

Steel True
Blade Straight

Epitaph on the gravestone of
Sir Arthur Conan Doyle
All Saints Churchyard
Minstead, England

ACT ONE

Prologue

*(We see two men alone in a room at the back of a tavern. One of them, **MIROSLAV HAČEK**, an agent of the Bohemian Police Force, is questioning an underworld criminal named **RUPERT PERKINS**.)*

HAČEK. Tell me who you work for.

PERKINS. I can't tell you.

HAČEK. Why not?

PERKINS. I'm frightened.

HAČEK. More frightened of him than of me?

PERKINS. Yes.

> *(BANG!)*

> *(**HAČEK** bangs on the table.)*

HAČEK. *YOU SHOULD NOT BE!*

PERKINS. *AHH!*

HAČEK. *TELL ME!*

PERKINS. *No! If I tell you, he'll kill my family!*

HAČEK. And I vill kill them *IF YOU DO NOT TELL ME!*

PERKINS. No. Please. He'll stop at nothing. If you are not loyal to him, then he...he's ruthless.

HAČEK. Tell me his name.

PERKINS. No.

HAČEK. *TELL ME!*

PERKINS. ...His name is...Moriarty. Professor James Moriarty.

HAČEK. Thank you. Now you vill tell me vhere to find him.

(**HAČEK** *turns away.* **PERKINS** *seizes his chance: he shoves a pill into his mouth, bites down and screams in agony.*)

PERKINS. *AGHHHHHHHH!*

HAČEK. *No! Stop it! Spit out the pill!*

PERKINS. *Agh!*

HAČEK. *We are not finished!*

PERKINS. *Agh! Agh!*

(**PERKINS** *falls to the ground, gasping for air, his body contorted, with rivers of foam spilling out of his mouth.*)

(**HAČEK** *looks on in astonishment.*)

HAČEK. Cyanide!

(*At which moment, the lights change, and we hear the disembodied, haunting voice of* **PROFESSOR MORIARTY** *intoning a single syllable into the darkness.*)

MORIARTY. Holmes...

(*The lights fade.*)

End of Prologue

Scene One: The Opera House

(We are at the Royal Opera House in Covent Garden, London, 1891. Onstage, Mimi and Rodolfo are singing La Bohème, *and in one of the boxes, we see* **SHERLOCK HOLMES**, *his head thrown back with a Byronic air, listening intently. Next to him is* **DOCTOR WATSON**, *and in a box on the other side of the auditorium sits* **IRENE ADLER**.*)*

(She is a raven-haired beauty of such intensity and irony that the very air around her seems shocked into stillness. **SHERLOCK HOLMES**, *as he absorbs the lushness of the sounds from the stage, sees* **MISS ADLER** *and stares at her with a look of curiosity. She glows with the intensity of a Greek goddess.)*

WATSON. *(To us.)* To Sherlock Holmes she was always *the* woman. I have seldom heard him mention her under any other name. In his eyes she eclipsed and predominated the whole of her sex.

(The voices on stage rise to beauty in the La Bohème *duet "O soave fanciulla."*)*

He first saw Miss Adler from his box at the Royal Opera House in Covent Garden. I happened to glance at him at the time and it was obvious that – quite uncharacteristically for a man who feared that emotion might ever interfere with his reason – he was smitten by her instantly.

At the time, he had no occasion to speak with her – nor did he during our frequent visits to the opera that

---

* A license to produce *KEN LUDWIG'S MORIARTY* does not include a performance license for any third-party or copyrighted recordings. Licensees should create their own.

season. But he would say, much later, after the case in question had reached its unexpected, shocking conclusion, that despite her beauty, or perhaps because of it, she was a woman destined for a tragic end.

> *(We hear the sounds of a London street of the period: the pleasant clip-clopping of the horses and the tolling of bells.)*

The case began on a cheerful sunlit morning at 221B Baker Street, the address I was sharing once again with Sherlock Holmes. My wife of four years had passed away suddenly in the Spring of that year, and I had moved back into our digs with a heavy heart that had at last begun to heal, in no small part thanks to the presence of my dear friend, Sherlock Holmes. To others he was a hero of great fame, but to me, he was simply my best friend.

> *(The scene changes to the drawing room of 221B Baker Street.)*

> *(221B is filled with sunlight streaming in through the windows. It is the room we have come to expect from all of the masterful stories and many of the adaptations of the Holmes and Watson canon. There are comfortable chairs, eccentric furnishings, letters stuck to the mantel with a jackknife, and evidence of chemical experiments on the desk. The room exudes the Sherlock Holmes we love to be with.)*

Scene Two: 221B Baker Street

(**HOLMES** *walks in wearing his dressing gown and greets the housekeeper and the scullery maid as usual.*)

HOLMES. Good morning, Mrs. Hudson. Daisy.

(**DAISY** *is the scullery maid in a mob cap, scrubbing the floor for dear life.*)

DAISY. G'morning, sir!

MRS. HUDSON. I hope you will have some breakfast this morning, Mr. Holmes. You are wasting away.

HOLMES. Mrs. Hudson, please don't obsess.

MRS. HUDSON. Oh, just look at you. You don't sleep at night. The house is filled with that foul tobacco smoke of yours, and you don't even open your mail anymore. Look at this. It arrived *yesterday*. It might be a client.

HOLMES. Of course it's a client.

MRS. HUDSON. You should open it.

HOLMES. I don't need to open it. I know perfectly well what it says by looking at the envelope.

WATSON. Oh come now, Holmes. That's going a bit far.

HOLMES. It is child's play, Watson.

MRS. HUDSON. For you, perhaps, because you're...well, you know who you are.

HOLMES. Mrs. Hudson. You have seen my methods a hundred times. Employ them yourself. This instant. What do you think?

MRS. HUDSON. Me?

HOLMES. Yes. Do your best. Something tells me you'll do quite well.

(She takes the envelope and examines it.)

MRS. HUDSON. Well... I-I-I think whoever wrote it is a... servant of some kind. Yes. A servant. And he works for a...nobleman. Or a king. That's it, he works for a king!

(She smells the envelope.)

And I think it's a king from one of those...exotic countries, like Silesia. No. Wrong. It's Bohemia. Yes. And he's coming this morning on urgent business, he'll be in a hurry, and don't be surprised if he's wearing *a black mask.* There. How's that? What do you think?!

HOLMES. I think you opened the letter this morning and read it.

MRS. HUDSON. Well of course I did, you silly man. How else could I possibly know all that.

*(**DAISY** laughs with delight.)*

WATSON. Well done, Mrs. Hudson.

DAISY. I hear a carriage arriving.

HOLMES. *(A glance out the window.)* And I see a pair of colts worth a hundred and fifty guineas apiece.

(We hear someone knocking at the front door.)

MRS. HUDSON. *I'm coming, I'm coming! Keep your shirt on!* Come along, Daisy. And Mr. Holmes, eat your breakfast.

*(**DAISY** giggles and they exit together.)*

WATSON. *(To us.)* This was the moment I cherished most. A sound on the stairs, a knock at the door and the sudden arrival of some new mystery.

(Knock knock!)

HOLMES. Enter, please.

(A giant of a man strides into the room. He is dressed richly in fur and silk, and he wears a black mask over his eyes. He surveys **HOLMES** *and* **WATSON** *intently.)*

THE MASKED MAN. *(With a harsh Bohemian accent.)* You haff had my note?

HOLMES. I have indeed. And you are –?

THE MASKED MAN. I am Count von Kramm, servant to the King of Bohemia, and you must promise me the utmost secrecy.

(To **WATSON.***)* You. Get out.

HOLMES. It is both or nothing.

THE MASKED MAN. I do not like it.

HOLMES. I don't like most things. Have a quince.

*(***HOLMES** *tosses him a quince, which he catches easily.)*

THE MASKED MAN. I do not vant a qvince!

HOLMES. Please be seated and tell me your problem.

THE MASKED MAN. I have come to you about some letters concerning a love affair that my master had with a Miss Irene Adler. The matter is now pressing because the King is about to marry a foreign princess, and if she knew about the King's affair, she would break off the engagement like that!

HOLMES. Which would of course have disastrous European results, don't you agree, your Majesty?

THE MASKED MAN. *(Spluttering.)* "Your-your-your *Majesty?*" How dare you qvestion me!

HOLMES. Oh come now, it's obvious that I'm speaking to King Otto of Bohemia, not his servant, his ambassador or the leader of his marching band, despite the size of the hat you're wearing.

THE MASKED MAN. *I am insulted! How dare you say such a thing!*

> *(He rips the hat from his head, takes a step towards* **HOLMES** *– and* **WATSON** *stands quickly and intervenes, instinctively protecting* **HOLMES**.*)*

WATSON. Sir!

> *(Beat. Then* **THE MASKED MAN** *stamps his foot and tears the mask from his face.)*

KING OTTO. How did you know?

HOLMES. Aside from your impatience, your expensive horses, and the signet ring you forgot to remove from your little finger, it is quite well-known that the hereditary line of Ormstein are all left-handed.

KING OTTO. The qvince.

HOLMES. The quince.

KING OTTO. Bah. I have come all the vay from Prague to consult you.

HOLMES. Then pray consult.

KING OTTO. You enrage me.

WATSON. He does that to most people.

> *(***KING OTTO** *takes a breath and begins:)*

KING OTTO. A year ago I made the acqvaintance of a beautiful American actress named Irene Adler and she turned my heart into somersaults.

HOLMES. And you wrote her some compromising letters and you want them back.

KING OTTO. *(Astonished.)* How do you know these things?

HOLMES. It is my business to know things. But tell me, how can anyone prove that the letters are real?

KING OTTO. The handwriting.

HOLMES. You could say it's a forgery.

KING OTTO. My note paper.

HOLMES. Say it was stolen.

KING OTTO. There is a photograph.

HOLMES. Oh.

KING OTTO. We are both in the photograph. In bed. In a highly unusual position.

WATSON. Oh dear.

KING OTTO. I vas mad – insane! But such is love, as you are no doubt avare.

HOLMES. I am not aware, but the photograph must be recovered.

KING OTTO. Of course it must! It is now with Miss Adler's sister. Her name is *Alice* Adler and she is held by people who are blackmailing me for a great sum of money.

HOLMES. I suggest you pay it.

KING OTTO. I vould pay anything! But they have gone silent, and my vedding is less than than a veek avay.

HOLMES. Do you know who they are?

KING OTTO. I have no idea. My agents say there is a man behind it who is known in criminal circles as Professor *Moriarty.*

(**HOLMES** *reacts. He is all attention.)*

HOLMES. You are certain of this?

KING OTTO. Yes, and they say he is terrifying. Last veek, my people had one of his henchmen cornered, but instead of answering all their qvestions, he bites on a pill and dies in front of them!

(**HOLMES** *is alert, his pulse racing. His questions are like darts of precision.*)

HOLMES. Where did this happen?

KING OTTO. In the back of a tavern.

HOLMES. Where?

KING OTTO. Does it matter?

HOLMES. *Where?*

KING OTTO. *In Cheapside, at the Bull and Bear, but vhy does it matter?!*

HOLMES. Do you know where the sister is being held?

KING OTTO. We think so. It is called Priory Cottage, in the village of Coulton in Cambridgeshire.

HOLMES. Excellent. Go. Now. I'll let you know when I can see you again.

KING OTTO. *(Spluttering.)* You will *"let me know"*? I am the King. I will not be dismissed by a mere –

HOLMES. *Get out! Now!*

(**KING OTTO** *stares furiously at* **HOLMES**, *then stamps his foot, gives a cry of anger and stalks out.*)

(*The light changes, and the room is suddenly dark and dangerous.*)

(*Time has stopped once again, and out of nowhere, we hear the voice of* **PROFESSOR MORIARTY***:*)

MORIARTY. *HOLMES.*

(**HOLMES** *looks up.* **WATSON** *doesn't hear it.*)

WATSON. Holmes. Holmes, what is it? What are you not telling me?

HOLMES. A great deal, but I'll explain on the train. Meet me at King's Cross, Platform Nine, in one hour and bring Cartwright and Milker with you. Have them pick up these items along the way.

(He scribbles a note.)

And Watson.

WATSON. Holmes?

HOLMES. Bring your revolver.

WATSON. *(To us.)* Within seconds, Holmes was in his chair, eyes closed, with his knees drawn under his chin, and I knew when he entered such a profound state, that I could have set off a bomb in the fireplace and he wouldn't have noticed. *Taxi...taxi!*

(And we're on the street.)

Scene Three: On Baker Street in the Rain

*(Two cockney lads of about fourteen appear
out of nowhere. They're cheerful, resourceful,
and competitive.)*

CARTWRIGHT. Hello, Doctor. No need to yell.

MILKER. We can get ya a taxi in seconds.

WATSON. Cartwright. Milker. How on earth did you know
I'd be here?

CARTWRIGHT. I dunno. I've got this kind o' sixth sense
where you and Mr. 'Olmes is concerned.

MILKER. I think me friend 'ere is whatcha call paranormal.

CARTWRIGHT. No, I'm not. I'm exotic.

MILKER. Freaky.

CARTWRIGHT. Prophetic.

MILKER. Peculiar.

CARTWRIGHT. Telepathic.

MILKER. Insane.

WATSON. Enough! We have a job for you.

CARTWRIGHT. Is it dangerous?

WATSON. Yes.

MILKER. Excellent.

CARTWRIGHT. Now I'll get ya that taxi ya wanted.

MILKER. *I'll* get it.

CARTWRIGHT. I said I'll do it.

MILKER. I'll do it faster.

CARTWRIGHT. Oh sure, you wish.

MILKER. Me da has a taxi.

CARTWRIGHT. Me ma has a carriage.

MILKER. And I've got a yacht.

CARTWRIGHT. And I got a balloon, two battleships and half an army!

WATSON. *Boys, that's enough!*

(*To us.*) On the way to the station, we stopped at Mrs. Gasner's Newsagents, Dry Goods, and Sundries and picked up the items that Holmes requested –

> (*The door opens with the tinkle of a bell.*
> **MRS. GASNER** *is efficiency itself and carries*
> *a clipboard.*)

MRS. GASNER. Come in, come in and state your business. Do not shilly-shally with a lot of nonsense, I'm a busy woman.

CARTWRIGHT. A quart o' paraffin.

MRS. GASNER. It's on the shelf.

MILKER. A wick.

MRS. GASNER. To the left.

CARTWRIGHT. And an empty bottle that holds exactly eight and a quarter ounces o' liquid when it's filled, not more nor less!

> (*Bang! There it is.*)

MRS. GASNER. Would you like to measure it, dearie, or take my word for it?

MILKER. Ha!

> (*The boys start to go.*)

MRS. GASNER. Ah-ah. Say the magic words.

MILKER & CARTWRIGHT. Thank you.

MRS. GASNER. Not those magic words, dearies. The ones that go "Here is your money *and I'm not going to stiff you for a change!*" We respectable women require a certain amount of upkeep, and don't you forget it.

CARTWRIGHT. Sorry.

MILKER. Sorry.

(They pay and leave.)

WATSON. We left Gasner's and arrived at King's Cross Station right on time. I could see Holmes on the platform waiting for us, and even at a distance I could tell that his eyes were ablaze with new purpose.

CONDUCTOR. *(Voiceover.) All aboard for Cambridge, stopping at Epping, Harlow and Great Shelford.*

Scene Four: Platform Nine at King's Cross Station

CARTWRIGHT. 'Allo, Mr. 'Olmes.

MILKER. It's good to see ya!

HOLMES. Cartwright. Milker.

(A rude **PORTER** *bustles past pushing a trolley.)*

PORTER. Porter! Porter! I'm comin' through!

CARTWRIGHT. Hey, be careful!

MILKER. Watch yer step!

(The **PORTER** *growls back.)*

CARTWRIGHT. So what's the case, Mr. Holmes?

HOLMES. The *case* is to listen to me very carefully. The doctor and I will be in Carriage Seven, Compartment Two, and Cartwright, I want you to patrol the carriage but remain invisible –

CARTWRIGHT. "Invisible."

HOLMES. And if anyone suspicious comes near my compartment, call out loudly. Do not approach him, he is likely to be extremely dangerous.

CARTWRIGHT. Yes sir.

MILKER. And what do *I* do, sir?

HOLMES. You will travel to the town of Grantchester outside Cambridge by a separate train, then double back to this address. Then at two o'clock precisely – do you hear me? –

MILKER. Two o'clock precisely!

HOLMES. – you will start a fire in the grate in the kitchen.

MILKER. You mean to cook the supper, sir?

HOLMES. No, to burn the house down.

MILKER & CARTWRIGHT. *All right!*

HOLMES. Did you stop at Gasner's?

CARTWRIGHT. Yes, sir. And we got them accessorieties you asked for.

MILKER. Paraffin.

CARTWRIGHT. Done.

MILKER. Wick.

CARTWRIGHT. Done.

MILKER. And an empty bottle. Are you makin' a table lamp?

HOLMES. No, a bomb.

MILKER & CARTWRIGHT. *Yes!*

> (*"Oweeeee!"*)

CONDUCTOR. *(Voiceover.) All aboard!*

> (*Chuggachuggachuggachuggachugga chugga.*)

Scene Five: Aboard the Train

WATSON. *(To us.)* Within a few minutes I found myself in the corner of our compartment, flying along en route to Great Shelford, while Sherlock Holmes, his sharp, eager face framed in his traveling cap, brooded in the opposite corner. As it turned out, it was one of the most important discussions of our lives.

HOLMES. ...Watson. I assume that you have never heard of Professor James Moriarty.

WATSON. Never.

HOLMES. And that is the genius of the man. He pervades London and no one has heard of him. That is what puts him on a pinnacle in the history of crime.

WATSON. Crime?

HOLMES. I tell you Watson, in all seriousness, if I could beat the man, I would gladly sacrifice myself in the process.

WATSON. Holmes, really... What has he done?

HOLMES. His career has been remarkable. At the age of twenty he wrote a treatise on the Binomial Theorem and had the Chair of Mathematics at Cambridge just two years later. But it turned out that he had tendencies of a criminal nature. Dark rumors gathered round him at the university and eventually he was compelled to leave.

WATSON. You weren't there at the time...?

HOLMES. Indeed I was. He was my mentor, and I worshipped him. We worked together, we dined together, we were as inseparable as Juno's swans. Then the rumors began and he started avoiding me. It was said that he'd committed the most atrocious crimes, all for money.

WATSON. That's monstrous.

HOLMES. At first I refused to believe it. But then one day I was in his office, and I found a letter in his handwriting. He was blackmailing another professor for his indiscretions.

WATSON. Good God.

HOLMES. He wanted money and he threatened violence. I was going to go to the police with the letter, but I… I hesitated. I convinced myself I needed more evidence. The truth is, I didn't want to confront him. I loved him and I was frightened of him.

WATSON. Of course you were. Anyone would have been.

HOLMES. I delayed for a week, and then I found it. *Proof after proof.* But alas, by the time I sought him out, he had fled. He got away! And it was my fault!

WATSON. Oh, come now. You can't blame yourself!

HOLMES. Oh I can. And then came the scandal, but it was too late. He was gone because of *me*. Because of my cowardice! Shortly after that, I received a letter, and in it, he admitted all he had done. He swore he would build an empire upon extortion, forgery, murder, anything to acquire power and wealth.

At that moment, I knew my calling. I would become a detective to stop such villainy and atone for my lack of courage. So oddly enough, it was Moriarty who made me what I have tried to become. *But I should have stopped him from the beginning and I failed to do it!*

WATSON. So stop him now. Track him down and have him arrested.

HOLMES. I have tried, Watson. He remains invisible. And yet, he is the seed of all that is evil in our great city. He sits motionless like a spider in the center of its web, and he knows the quiver of every thread. *He is the Napoleon of Crime!*

WATSON. But what can you do? You need him to slip.

HOLMES. Aha. Yes. I do. *And I think he has.*

WATSON. How?

HOLMES. *(His eyes gleam with a new light.) The King's letters.* We are on to him early on this one. And it is just possible if we move quickly we can stop him forever. Now listen carefully, I have a plan.

> *(As they huddle together, we see* **CARTWRIGHT** *patrolling the corridor. After a beat, a* **VICAR** *with a clerical collar enters, engrossed in a crossword puzzle.)*

VICAR. Seven down. A three-letter palindrome denoting surprise.

> *(Showing him the puzzle.)*

CARTWRIGHT. Wow.

VICAR. "Wow."

> *(Writing it down.)*

Oh very good. Well done, young man.

> *(He exits, passing the* **PORTER** *we met on the platform.)*

PORTER. Porter! Porter! I'm comin' through!

CARTWRIGHT. Oy. 'Ow's business?

PORTER. What's it to you?

CARTWRIGHT. You was the porter in the station, remember? But wait a sec. I thought porters stayed *in* the station, so what're ya doin' here in the –...

> *(Just as* **CARTWRIGHT** *realizes the implications of this: Wham! The* **PORTER** *slams* **CARTWRIGHT** *against the window and starts to strangle him.)*

CARTWRIGHT. *AGH!*

PORTER. *Lit'le smart-aleck. I'll kill you first, then get to Holmes.*

> (*As he strangles* **CARTWRIGHT**, *we see* **HOLMES** *and* **WATSON** *in the compartment, oblivious to the fight going on behind them:*)

WATSON. Holmes, I think your plan is ingenious.

HOLMES. We'll see if it works. And now let's write some love letters, shall we?

WATSON. "Love letters"?

HOLMES. From the King to Miss Adler. The decoys.

WATSON. Oh right, right, right. Of course. The plan.

> (**HOLMES** *takes out a pen and paper and begins forging a set of the King's letters. Meanwhile:*)

CARTWRIGHT. *Agh! Agh!*

PORTER. *Stop squirmin', ya little snake...*

> (*The* **PORTER** *strangles* **CARTWRIGHT** *with one hand, and he opens the outside train door with the other; we see the countryside shooting past at about 100 miles an hour.* **CARTWRIGHT** *fights for his life, and the* **PORTER** *tries to shove him through the door.*)

CARTWRIGHT. *No!*

> (*As the* **PORTER** *tries to shove* **CARTWRIGHT** *through the door, the* **VICAR** *walks by, engrossed in his puzzle.*)

VICAR. Four letter word for desperation, often followed by an exclamation point.

CARTWRIGHT. *HELP!*

VICAR. Oh, excellent! What a brain.

> *(The **VICAR** exits, filling in his crossword puzzle, as **CARTWRIGHT** fights for his life. Then he turns the tables and **CARTWRIGHT** shoves the **PORTER** out the door – and the **PORTER** shoots down the side of the train to certain death.)*

PORTER. *AHHHHHHHHHHHHHH!*

CONDUCTOR. *(Voiceover.)* Great Shelford! All out for Great Shelford!

> *(As the train pulls to a stop, **HOLMES** and **WATSON** exit the compartment, passing **CARTWRIGHT** who is disheveled, panting, and heaving with exhaustion.)*

HOLMES. Cartwright. Stop the tomfoolery and come on!

> *(As they leave the train, the stage darkens and we hear the frightening, discordant opening of Mahler's Third Symphony.*)*
>
> *(Then suddenly a bright light is shining directly at us, nearly blinding us, and we're in...)*

---

* A license to produce *KEN LUDWIG'S MORIARTY* does not include a performance license for any third-party or copyrighted recordings. Licensees should create their own.

Scene Six: Moriarty's Lair

(An underground room, full of dirty pipes and dripping water. A tough, pugnacious woman named **MRS. BARABAS** *strides in. She has a chip on her shoulder and is dressed to match. She tries to see behind the light and shields her eyes from the glare.)*

MRS. BARABAS. Professor? Is that you, Professor?

(We hear **PROFESSOR MORIARTY**'s *voice, but we don't see him. His voice echoes.)*

MORIARTY. Yes, Mrs. Barabas. Please report.

MRS. BARABAS. Right. All right. Got it. So this girl, ya see, named Alice Adler is in me custody, as you might call it, inside the house, and I got the King's letters and they're in the safe. How d'ya like *that*?

MORIARTY. But?

MRS. BARABAS. But nothin'. They're in the safe and they're locked up.

MORIARTY. *BUT?*

MRS. BARABAS. But I'm still missin' the combination. She changed the numbers, the little witch.

MORIARTY. She changed the combination of the safe?

MRS. BARABAS. Don't sound so worried-like. I got the best man in the business on it, Mr. Paddy Keys, and he'll have it open in minutes from now, it's guaranteed.

MORIARTY. So Miss Adler may in fact *have* the letters.

MRS. BARABAS. No, no, she does not! Ya see, I searched the bleedin' house from top to bottom, and she never *left* the house, so they gotta be there *in* the house. D'ya get it now?!

(A low rumble in the score.)

MORIARTY. Don't disappoint me, Mrs. Barabas. There will be consequences.

MRS. BARABAS. Disappoint you? Ain't you listenin'? I got the best man in the business on it –

(Bang! A door slams shut. Silence. To herself:)

"Consequences." I know all about consequences, thank you very m–...

(She has tried to open the door and it's locked.)

Hey, what's this? Open the door, d'ya hear me? *Open the door!*

(Rattling the door in desperation.)

YOU STOP IT RIGHT NOW, YA HEAR ME?!

(Click. The door is unlocked from the other side. She opens the door, breathes a sigh of relief –)

Well bloody thank you.

(She runs out of the room, her heart racing –)

Scene Seven: The Drawing Room of Priory Cottage

*(...and bursts through the front door of Priory Cottage where we see **PADDY KEYS**, a lively criminal out of Damon Runyon, trying to open the safe.)*

MRS. BARABAS. Well? Well? Did ya get it open?!

PADDY. Patience, me girl. Ya wouldn't rush Mickey Angelo when he was a-paintin' the Cistern Chapel, would ya?

MRS. BARABAS. Well o' course I –

PADDY. Shh! ...Got it!

(The safe opens with a click.)

MRS. BARABAS. Yes. *Yes!* Oh, thank ya, God.

PADDY. Uh oh.

MRS. BARABAS. What?

PADDY. Not good.

MRS. BARABAS. What?!

PADDY. The safe is empty.

MRS. BARABAS. ...Empty?

(She stoops and puts her hand inside.)

It's empty. The bleedin' safe is bleedin' gya goh ga k-k-k-gya gya ghhhhhaaaaaaaaaa!

(She's having a crisis.)

Get the girl down here! Go! NOW!

*(**PADDY** runs up the stairs, while **MRS. BARABAS** bangs on the safe and has a fit. Then he comes back down with a modest,*

blonde young woman named **ALICE ADLER**.
*She's a beautiful young thing, eyes downcast,
in a lovely dress, her hair tumbling to her
shoulders. She speaks quietly in a southern
American accent.)*

You! Where are the letters?!

ALICE. They're in the safe, I believe.

MRS. BARABAS. No, they're not in the safe. They're not in
the bloody empty safe and you know it. Now where the
bloody hell are they?!

ALICE. I'm afraid I can't tell you.

MRS. BARABAS. Oh you're gonna tell me all right or I'll –

(Grabbing her wrist and twisting it violently.)

ALICE. *Ahhh.* They belong to my sister. I can't. I can't tell
you. Please.

*(Bing bong! The front doorbell sounds, and
they freeze.)*

MRS. BARABAS. See who it is. And *you,* keep your voice
down.

*(**PADDY** opens the door a crack, sees who it is,
then slams it shut.)*

PADDY. Jaysus, Mary and Joseph. It's Sherlock Holmes.

MRS. BARABAS. What?

PADDY. *The detective! Sherlock Holmes! The one who
solves all the cases! Don't ya ever read the paper!*

(Bing bong!)

MRS. BARABAS. Oh, *him.* I know all about him. He can't do
any harm. And remember, my name is Mrs. Chetwood
while I'm here. And *you,* you keep yer mouth shut.

(**HOLMES** *enters.*)

HOLMES. Good afternoon. You are –?

MRS. BARABAS. Mrs. Ethel Chetwood, what's it to you?

HOLMES. I'm here to see Miss Alice Adler. May I presume that the young woman whose wrist you are holding so forcefully is indeed Miss Adler?

ALICE. Yes, I am.

MRS. BARABAS. As you can see, the poor thing's a invalid. I've got to hold her up. Ha!

HOLMES. Perhaps she's confined to the house too much.

MRS. BARABAS. Oh, ain't you the funny one. I know about you and I ain't impressed. And I suppose you know about me already from all those clues you pretend to pick up out o' nothin'. Go ahead! What do you know?!

HOLMES. (*Without taking his eyes from her.*) Nothing of consequence, I'm afraid, except that your real name is Athena Barabas, as the envelope on the desk tells us. You served time at Dartmoor Prison where you got that snake tattoo on your wrist. And you're holding this woman against her will, for which I could have you arrested by the policeman I see through the window walking down the street. Madam, may I be of assistance to you?

ALICE. I'm...I'm all right. But why are you here?

HOLMES. My name is Sherlock Holmes and my client wishes to obtain certain letters written by him to your sister, Miss Irene Adler, which I believe are now in your possession.

ALICE. It is true that I have such letters, Mr. Holmes, but it will be impossible to get them away from me. Others have tried and failed.

HOLMES. What others have done or not done is of no consequence to me, Miss Adler. I am here on behalf of my client, the King of Bohemia, who asks your sister for forgiveness.

ALICE. He doesn't deserve it. This is all his fault and he must pay for it!

HOLMES. Are you sure of this?

ALICE. I'm positive.

HOLMES. Then your answer is final?

ALICE. I'm afraid it is.

HOLMES. *(Consulting his pocket watch.)* Well look at the time. It appears to be two o'clock precisely.

(Silence.)

Two o'clock precisely.

(Silence.)

Two o'clock precisely!

(BOOM! We hear an explosion, then a police whistle, then cries of "Fire! Fire!" by members of the public.)

MRS. BARABAS. Holy goddam!

PADDY. What was that?!

MRS. BARABAS. It came from the kitchen!

PADDY. The house is on fire!

*(As **MRS. BARABAS** and **PADDY** run out, **ALICE** makes a move towards an upholstered ottoman. The moment she does, she realizes that she has betrayed her hiding place for the letters.)*

ALICE. No!

HOLMES. Please don't alarm yourself, Miss Adler. There is no fire. I simply wanted to know where you'd hidden the letters.

> *(He rips open the upholstery and pulls out the letters.)*

I hope you'll forgive me.

> *(Her entire demeanor has changed instantly, and suddenly she speaks with a new American accent – not Southern, but her own voice.)*

ALICE. Of course I won't forgive you, you stuck-up, pompous idiot.

HOLMES. I beg your pardon?

ALICE. I had her eating out of my hand. I had her terrified and now you've ruined everything!

HOLMES. What? What are you talking about?

ALICE. The letters! I need those letters so I can flush out a man named Professor James Moriarty and kill him!

HOLMES. But why?

ALICE. Because he – ...oh, none of your business. Just – ... Oh my God, she's coming back, you fool!

HOLMES. Wait. Here. Hide the originals. We'll give her these instead.

ALICE. They're counterfeit?

HOLMES. Yes they're counterfeit. I prepared them on the train, but they'll have to do. Quickly. Quickly!

> *(As **ALICE** hides the real papers, **MRS. BARABAS** walks in with her gun drawn. **HOLMES**, on purpose, is holding out the counterfeit papers.)*

MRS. BARABAS. Stop right there and put 'em up. Mr. Sherlock Holmes. Now hand 'em over!

HOLMES. *(Acting, but not very well.)* Damn. You got me.

ALICE. *(Also acting.)* Oh no. Please Mr. Holmes. Don't let her have the papers.

HOLMES. But what can I do? She's outsmarted both of us.

MRS. BARABAS. Outsmarted is right. Got 'em!

> *(She grabs the papers from **HOLMES**, at which moment, **WATSON** hurries in.)*

WATSON. Holmes, I just wanted to confirm that you're all – ...Good God.

HOLMES. Stay back, Watson. The woman's a genius. She's bested all of us.

MRS. BARABAS. You're bloody right, I have. And I'm takin' these straight to Professor Moriarty. Hahaaaa!

> *(She runs out.)*

ALICE. *(Dropping her Southern accent again, this time for good.)* Good luck with that.

HOLMES. Watson. Miss Alice Adler.

WATSON. How do you do.

ALICE. Not well at all, and I am not Alice Adler.

> *(She pulls off her blonde wig and shakes out her striking dark hair and is suddenly transformed into a whole new woman.)*

My name is Irene Adler. I'm Alice's sister.

WATSON. Good God. From the opera.

ALICE/IRENE. I beg your pardon?

HOLMES. We have seen you at Covent Garden on several occasions.

IRENE. Oh. That was you. You were staring at me.

HOLMES. Was I?

WATSON. Incessantly.

HOLMES. Watson.

(*To* **IRENE.**) But why are you here?

IRENE. I'm here to track down a man named Moriarty and kill him. What about you?

WATSON. About the same, I believe.

HOLMES. Miss Adler, we have a great deal to discuss. Will you join us at Baker Street for a few days?

WATSON. Baker Street!

HOLMES. For her safety.

IRENE. Fine! I will if you don't make any more bone-headed mistakes. But remember, Moriarty is mine.

(**IRENE** *strides from the room.*)

HOLMES. American.

WATSON. Well, obviously, but Baker Street?

(*To us:*) I will admit to being shocked and quite suddenly...jealous. I know it was irrational, but there it was: my best friend forging a new alliance. We had a guest room of course, but still.

Also, I couldn't help wondering what happened to Mrs. Barabas when she gave the Professor the counterfeit packet of letters that Holmes had prepared.

(*We hear a blood-curdling scream from* **MRS. BARABAS.**)

MRS. BARABAS. (*Offstage.*) *AHHHHHHHH!*

WATSON. That morning, in Baker Street, Mrs. Hudson was in a state of shock.

Scene Eight: 221B Baker Street

> (**MRS. HUDSON** *appears, her mouth agape, as though Martians just landed in her drawing room.*)

MRS. HUDSON. Dr. Watson. He brought home a woman.

WATSON. Indeed he has.

MRS. HUDSON. A woman! At his age. He's over forty! And he says she can sleep in the spare bedroom! I haven't changed the sheets in that room since the Crimean War.

> (**HOLMES** *enters in his dressing gown.*)

HOLMES. Good morning, Mrs. Hudson. Thank you for taking care of Miss Adler. I'm certain she appreciates it.

IRENE. *(Offstage.) There's no hot water in this house! How can you live in a house with no hot water?! It's like the Middle Ages!*

MRS. HUDSON. *(Hurrying out.)* Oh dear.

WATSON. Things got even more complicated when Miss Adler realized she no longer possessed the King's letters.

IRENE. *(Offstage.) Mr. Holmes, are you a common THIEF?*

WATSON. Our cat Nefertiti was so frightened she jumped out the window.

NEFERTITI. *Meeeeeooooowww.*

WATSON. Neffie!

IRENE. *(Entering.)* Mr. Holmes, your client, Otto von Ormstein, sent those letters directly to me, which is why I own them!

HOLMES. Wrong. The letters belong to my client who wrote them.

IRENE. Wrong. They were in my possession.

HOLMES. Wrong. The case is Chase versus *The Telegraph,* September 1890, Civil Division.

IRENE. *Well who the hell cares?* And how did you get them? I was sleeping with them. They were tucked in my nightgown.

HOLMES. I apologize. It was dark, I assure you.

IRENE. You hypocrite. Sherlock Holmes, the great detective, who has never even looked at a woman except when she drops her lace handkerchief.

HOLMES. You're a challenging person.

IRENE. Because I'm right, now give them back.

HOLMES. Why are they so important to you? You promised to discuss it this morning. I'm waiting.

IRENE. Oh, fine. It's not the letters themselves that are important. It's Moriarty. Yes, I had a...friendship with Otto while I was on the Continent. We shared a bed. Does that shock you?

HOLMES. No.

IRENE. I didn't know he was royalty, we just liked each other. I went back to London, he wrote me some letters, and some people found out about them. They tried to buy them from me, and when I said no, it turned into threats, so I thought it best to hide the letters, and I sent them to my sister Alice back in America.

Then somehow these...these *people* found out about them, and they went to her and tried to *get* the letters and they

(*Her voice falters.*)

I suppose they got angry and they...they killed her. *THEY KILLED MY SISTER.*

(*She breaks down in tears.*)

THEY KILLED MY SISTER FOR A PACKET OF LETTERS!

> *(She flings herself onto* **HOLMES***'s chest and weeps.* **HOLMES** *has no idea what to do with his arms.)*

Sorry. Stupid.

HOLMES. Did the police find anyone?

IRENE. No one. Nothing. So I've spent the past several months trying to find out who they are and it's led me to the man I mentioned. His name is James Moriarty and he was a professor of mathematics. That's all I know.

HOLMES. It's all anyone knows.

IRENE. Then you've heard of him?

HOLMES. He's a monster. What I *don't* understand is why he wants the letters so desperately. Oh yes of course he can blackmail the King and there's money in it. But he blackmails people every day. There must be something else in the letters that only he is aware of.

IRENE. Have you met him?

HOLMES. Yes indeed.

IRENE. Do you know where to find him?

HOLMES. No idea, which is infuriating.

IRENE. Then what do we do now?

HOLMES. "We"?

IRENE. Yes, we! I lost a sister, so don't pretend I'm not involved in this, now what do we *do*?

HOLMES. ...My goal is to flush him out, and to do it I need to find his *list*.

IRENE. What list?

HOLMES. A list of all his confederates around the country. I have learned that he carries it exclusively on his person, in his coat pocket. Once I find it, my plan is to alert Scotland Yard, then coordinate a series of arrests, one at a time but very quickly, so that he doesn't know what hit him. He will see the circle closing around him relentlessly, he will panic, and *I will have him!*

IRENE. You seem obsessed with the man.

HOLMES. I don't have obsessions.

IRENE. Ha!

HOLMES. I beg your pardon.

IRENE. Do you always set your sights so high?

HOLMES. Yes.

IRENE. As do I. In everything?

HOLMES. Yes.

> *(Now he is talking about her, and they both know it.)*
>
> *(****WATSON**** enters. He sees the intimacy of the look between **HOLMES** and **IRENE** and he is slightly taken aback.)*

WATSON. Excuse me, Holmes. Sorry to "bother" you. But you won't believe who's at the door right now.

HOLMES. Tell me.

WATSON. Your brother Mycroft.

HOLMES. Good God.

IRENE. Why the astonishment?

HOLMES. He hasn't left the Diogenes Club in two years. A planet might as well leave its orbit. I'll see what he wants.

(**HOLMES** *exits.*)

IRENE. He has a brother? There are two of them?

WATSON. Yes, of course. He appears in my chronicles in the *Strand Magazine*. Don't you read them?

IRENE. I'm afraid I haven't.

WATSON. Oh.

IRENE. Sorry. I didn't mean to insult you. I've heard that the stories are marvelous. And very touching.

WATSON. Thank you. I will admit I put my heart and soul into them. Anyway, Holmes does have a brother, Mycroft, who is equally brainy, if not more so.

IRENE. Is he also distant?

WATSON. Yes. Though I doubt if anyone is quite as distant as Holmes.

IRENE. So I noticed. Whenever I try to provoke him, he puts on those hooded eyes of his and chews on his pipe. I told him there was no hot water in the house and it was unacceptable, and all he said was: *(Imitating Holmes.)* "You are presumably a grown woman, so learn to deal with it." *How do you talk to a man like that?!*

WATSON. We are old friends. We have our own language.

IRENE. Well, teach me some. I have a feeling he's worth knowing.

WATSON. Oh he is, I promise.

IRENE. Is it a deal?

WATSON. Deal.

(*They shake hands.*)

Would you like to meet his brother, Mycroft?

IRENE. I sure would. Thanks. I'll join you in a minute.

(She sweeps away.)

WATSON. *(To us.)* I found the brothers in the parlor, as different and yet as similar as they could possibly be.

Scene Nine: 221B Baker Street

*(The sitting room. SHERLOCK and MYCROFT
are in conference. MYCROFT is a man of
massive frame with a suggestion of uncouth
physical inertia. "But above his unwieldy
frame there is perched a head so masterful in
its brow, so alert in its steely-grey, deep-set
eyes, so firm in its lips, and so subtle in its
play of expression, that after one glance one
forgets the gross body and remembers only
the dominant mind.")*

MYCROFT. I tell you I need to see the letters first.

HOLMES. And I'm merely asking you why they're important.

MYCROFT. I will tell you as soon as you hand them over.

HOLMES. And I'll hand them over as soon as you tell me.

MYCROFT. That will be a first.

HOLMES. Oh please. My life is spent doing your bidding.

MYCROFT. It certainly is not.

HOLMES. Of course it is.

MYCROFT. You are preposterous.

HOLMES. You are provoking.

MYCROFT. You are galling.

HOLMES. You are absurd.

WATSON. When they were together, they became children
again. It was like watching Tweedledee and Tweedledum.

(**IRENE** *enters, looking ravishing.*)

IRENE. Hello, gentlemen.

HOLMES. Miss Adler. This is my brother Mycroft.

MYCROFT. How do you do.

HOLMES. He wants to see the King's letters –

MYCROFT. Which I need as a matter of state business. I work for the British government.

WATSON. At times, he is the British government.

HOLMES. But I refuse to show them to him.

IRENE. The point is moot because you don't have the letters.

HOLMES. Of course I have them. I took them last night in your sleep, remember?

IRENE. And I took them back a moment ago.

HOLMES. That's impossible. They're in my safe.

IRENE. Not anymore.

HOLMES. Good God. The letters! Let me see those. I locked them up.

IRENE. And I burgled them.

MYCROFT. What an extraordinary woman.

IRENE. Are you as clever as your brother?

MYCROFT. Yes, and he freely admits it. But he's a bit of a show-off with his parlor games.

IRENE. His deductions, you mean.

MYCROFT. Yes, and of course they're all quite simple. I could do them all day. He is transparent.

IRENE. *(Laughing.)* Yes, I know.

HOLMES. I beg your pardon?

IRENE. *(Ignoring* **SHERLOCK.***)* Now what can you deduce about me? A mere Highland Mary.

MYCROFT. Aha. That was a clue. You're testing me. Wicked woman. Well, let's see. Your parents emigrated to North

America and you grew up initially in Canada, then moved to the Southern portion of the United States. It's all in the vowels. From there you travelled, mostly in England where you were educated. You wear a watch chain like an English barrister – I saw you glance at it. You value education and you studied in Scotland, hence the Burns quotation. You also spent time in New York City, and that I deduce from your cheekiness.

IRENE. Anything else?

MYCROFT. You're a fencer. Witness the marks on your dominant hand. Épée or Sabre?

IRENE. Sabre.

MYCROFT. Naturally. And of course you're a Jewess. I assure you I say that with admiration. You wear a Star of David, made in Odessa, so your parents no doubt fought the Cossacks and fled the pogroms.

IRENE. It's a point of pride.

MYCROFT. I should hope so. The Holmes family is over one-quarter Jewish and I'm sure it's why my brother is so deeply attracted to you.

HOLMES. *(Annoyed.)* May we stick to business, please.

MYCROFT. *(To* **IRENE.***)* I've embarrassed him, which is such a pleasure. May I see the letters?

IRENE. Why do you want them so badly?

MYCROFT. I want to look for a secret they harbor of national importance.

(**IRENE** *hands* **MYCROFT** *the letters.)*

IRENE. I'm afraid you're going to be disappointed. I've read the letters a hundred times and there's nothing in them but –

MYCROFT. Indiscretions? Oh I wouldn't be so certain, my dear. I suspect at least one of them contains a microdot.

> (**MYCROFT** *holds one of the sheets up to the light. He examines it closely. He turns the sheet to the side and peers straight down it. He feels the edges. He feels the surface.*)

HOLMES. A microdot. I should have thought of it.

WATSON. What's a microdot?

IRENE. It's a tiny disc, about a millimeter in diameter, usually composed of a photograph.

> (**SHERLOCK** *looks at* **IRENE** *with renewed fascination.*)

WATSON. A photograph?

HOLMES. There are rumors afoot that a copy of the Bruce-Partington plans have been photographed and are up for sale.

IRENE. What are *they*?

MYCROFT. They are plans for a fleet of submarines that are able to carry bombs of enormous power, capable of destroying half of London in less than an hour.

WATSON. But how are the letters involved?

MYCROFT. The plans were hidden for a time in the Bohemian Embassy and we now surmise that there is a traitor at the embassy who obtained access to the plans some time ago. But because the plans are so large they couldn't be smuggled out the door.

WATSON. So they were photographed and put on a micro-something.

HOLMES. Dot.

IRENE. Which was put on one of Otto's letters by the traitor. And now Moriarty wants to retrieve the letters to obtain the plans.

MYCROFT. Exactly. May I take a look?

IRENE. I'll need them back.

MYCROFT. Of course.

> (**MYCROFT** *pulls out a pair of surgical loupes, i.e. glasses with tubes in front for magnification.*)

HOLMES. I have my own pair, thank you so much.

> (**SHERLOCK** *and* **MYCROFT** *both put the glasses on – and they look tremendously odd, like something from outer space. They waggle their heads at each other and laugh with boyish amusement. Then they split up the packet of letters and scan the pages. Things turn serious.*)

MYCROFT. Nothing.

HOLMES. Nothing.

MYCROFT. Nothing.

HOLMES. Not here.

MYCROFT. Nothing.

HOLMES. Wait. Ha ha! Look at this!

> (*He takes a pair of tweezers from his pocket and carefully picks something off one of the letters.*)

We'll do this very carefully... Don't move... *Got it.*

> (**MYCROFT** *takes out of his pocket a small viewer. It's about three inches long, like a jeweler's loupe, with a small handle.*)

MYCROFT. A Stanhope Viewer.

HOLMES. Please.

(**SHERLOCK** *turns over a wine glass and puts
the microdot on the flat surface of the base.
Then* **MYCROFT**, *using the Stanhope Viewer,
examines the contents of the microdot.)*

WATSON. This is rather exciting...

IRENE. I agree!

HOLMES. ...Anything?

MYCROFT. ...No, I don't see anything yet... Wait, wait... No.
Aha! This is it! There are diagrams and calculations.
It goes on for *pages.*

ALL. Ha haaa!! / Got it! / We're in business! / Yes!

*(They all embrace. Pure joy. It's like the "Rain
in Spain" moment in* My Fair Lady.)

WATSON. *(To us.)* It was like a party, and it was a pleasure
seeing Holmes joining right in. He had not been this
happy in a long time.

IRENE. Look, look! I've found another!

MYCROFT. Oh, excellent! Well done, young woman!

(The lights fade.)

WATSON. *(To us.)* Mycroft was fascinated by Miss Adler,
and I could see that Holmes was jealous, a feeling I
had never seen him experience before. It was rather a
pleasure seeing him entering the human race. An hour
later, Holmes, Miss Adler, and I took a walk to the
Bohemian Embassy to find the traitor.

Scene Ten: A Street in London

(The three are walking together in the bright sunlight of a clear London afternoon.)

WATSON. *(Continued.)* As we passed within a block of Regent's Park, I noticed that Holmes was glancing over his shoulder.

HOLMES. I believe we're being followed.

WATSON. *(Turning round.)* Really? Where?

HOLMES. Don't look.

WATSON. Sorry. Who is it do you think?

HOLMES. From his size and gait, I'd say it's Sebastian Moran.

IRENE. Who's Sebastian Moran?

HOLMES. He's Moriarty's number two. He's known primarily for his skill as a marksman – he hunts big game, he's a deadly shot – and he's suspected of several prominent murders here in London.

WATSON. Oh right, right, right. I've read about him in the Police Gazette.

IRENE. Do you think he was sent by Moriarty?

HOLMES. Without a doubt.

WATSON. You should arrest him then.

HOLMES. On what charge? Skulking down the street suspiciously?

WATSON. That's good enough for me! I'd clap him in irons! Look. He's still there.

IRENE. Where?

WATSON. Right there.

HOLMES. Don't look!

WATSON. Sorry.

IRENE. Sorry.

> *(Whispering.)*

What does he want?

HOLMES. He wants to kill you.

IRENE. Oh.

> *(They've arrived at the large, gleaming door of the embassy. **HOLMES** rings the bell.)*

> *(Bing bong!)*

Scene Eleven: On the Steps of the Bohemian Embassy

*(The door is opened by **HILDA**, the housekeeper. She eats barbed wire for breakfast and has a perpetual scowl on her face.)*

HILDA. *Bohemian Embassy. Vhat?*

IRENE. Hello, Hilda.

HILDA. *You. You are the voman who broke King Otto's heart und I could kill you mitt my bare hands!*

(Bang! She slams the door in their faces.)

IRENE. …She never liked me much.

HOLMES. Really? I wouldn't have guessed. Let's try again, shall we? I'll do the talking.

(Bing Bong!)

(The door opens again.)

HILDA. *VHAT?*

HOLMES. How do you do. I'm a consulting detective and I'm here on a vital mission that I was hired to do by the man you call –

(Bang! The door is slammed again.)

IRENE. That worked beautifully.

WATSON. May I give it a try?

HOLMES. Yes.

IRENE. Please.

(Bing Bong! The door opens again.)

HILDA. *VHAT?!*

WATSON. That dress you're wearing. Where did you get it? It's stunning on you.

HILDA. Please come in.

(As they follow her into the house, **WATSON** *whispers to* **HOLMES***:)*

WATSON. Human nature.

Scene Twelve: The Grand Hall

(As they walk into the main hall, we hear the grand opening theme of Wagner's Die Meistersinger.*)*

HILDA. Dis is der Main Hallvay of der embassy, und every single item dat you see vas made by a Bohemian artist. Bohemian chandelier by Krupkin. Bohemian vallpaper by Daggstadt. Bohemian *Mona Lisa* by Blaznik.

WATSON. And I imagine you did some of the decorating.

HILDA. You are very observant.

WATSON. You are kind to say so. If I am observant it's because my friend here is a detective. His name is –

HILDA. *I know his name! Und I know that he is helping the King get back his letters from this awful voman! I am told everything!*

(Walk, walk.)

IRENE. It's nice to see you again, Hilda.

HILDA. Don't tell me nice. You broke my master's heart into pieces vithout thinking tvice about it.

IRENE. Except he's the one getting married.

HILDA. *Because you are common person. You are nobody. He is King. And he is best man in entire vorld. Enter his study.*

Scene Thirteen: The King's Study

(They enter the King's palatial study, bright sunlight streams through a large floor-to-ceiling window looking out on Regent's Park. The room sparkles.)

HILDA. *(Continued.)* This is famous room. It is vhere King *thinks* und *vorks*. This is the picture vindow vhere he looks out at the vorld and gets great thoughts. If you touch anything in this room I vill kill you.

(To **WATSON.***)* Except for you, you may touch anything.

(She clicks her heels.)

(To all of them.) I get the King. Vait here.

(She exits, closing the door behind her.)

IRENE. *(Sighs.)* I spent many happy days in this house.

HOLMES. I'm sure you did.

IRENE. Don't be catty. Otto is the kindest man I've ever met. We'd have lunch right here at the window, overlooking the park.

(There is an elegant table with two chairs in front of the window, and **IRENE** *sits on one of them.)*

Surprisingly, we had a lot in common. And we were wildly attracted to each other.

And now I simply wish him well with his princess, which isn't his fault –

*(***HOLMES** *notices a glint of light through the window.)*

*(***HOLMES,** *without moving, says in a quiet, even tone of voice:)*

HOLMES. Don't move.

WATSON. Sorry?

(There's another glint of light through the window. We hear a tremolo in the score.)

HOLMES. Watson, pull the curtain.

WATSON. What? Sorry?

HOLMES. *(Firmly and evenly.) Pull the curtain across the window.*

WATSON. Oh I see. Moran. Right. And he doesn't know the microdots are no longer on the letters –

HOLMES. *Watson. PULL THE CURTAIN!*

WATSON. Got it.

*(***WATSON*** pulls the curtains and we heave a sigh of relief.)*

IRENE. You don't think that man with the gun is out there...?

HOLMES. Of course I do.

IRENE. But shooting me wouldn't get him the letters.

HOLMES. It would if they have someone in the embassy to search your dead body.

(At which moment, the doors are thrown open with a bang and **KING OTTO** *enters.)*

KING OTTO. *Brouček.*

IRENE. Otto.

KING OTTO. My darlink friend.

(He strides to **IRENE** *and they embrace.)*

Oh. You look so beautiful! And how I have missed you, it is so unfair.

IRENE. I know it is.

KING OTTO. I swear to you it iss not my fault. I am bullied and nagged all the time by my people.

IRENE. Yes, I know.

KING OTTO. The marriage to the princess, it is

IRENE. political.

KING OTTO. Yes. To preserve

IRENE. the peace. I know. And I have a surprise for you.

> *(She takes out the letters and offers them to* **KING OTTO.***)*

These are yours. The letters. I'm returning them. Including the photo.

> *(***KING OTTO*** is dumbstruck.)*

KING OTTO. Oh, Irene.

> *(He embraces her.)*

> *(***HOLMES*** senses something untoward and takes a step forward –)*

HOLMES. Wait. There's something wrong.

IRENE. Oh, I'm sure that you're exagger–

> *(BANG! A gunshot! The noise is explosive.)*

> *(The bullet tears through the curtains and through a lamp which explodes.)*

HOLMES. ON THE FLOOR! NOW!

IRENE. OTTO!

HOLMES. DOWN!

> *(He tackles* **IRENE** *to get her to the floor.)*

(BANG!)

*(The second bullet hits **KING OTTO** and he sprawls forward. There is blood everywhere.)*

IRENE. OTTO!

*(At which moment, the door opens, and **HILDA** enters. She sees **KING OTTO** covered in blood and screams.)*

HILDA. *AHHHHHH!*

IRENE. ...He's dead.

HILDA. *AHHHHHHHHHHH!*

(A light comes up on the King's letters, scattered on the floor.)

*(Then the voice of **MORIARTY** returns and echoes through the room.)*

MORIARTY. *HOLMES...*

(Blackout.)

End of Act One

ACT TWO

Scene One: The King's Study

WATSON. *(To us.)* With the death of King Otto von Ormstein, a case that began with a packet of letters took on new urgency. Within an hour of the King's demise, the embassy was swarming with members of the Foreign Service, as well as reporters from every newspaper in the land.

> *(We hear the sounds and see the flashbulbs of a gaggle of London reporters trying to get the story: "Do you have a lead?" "Is there a suspect?" "Who else was hurt?")*

Meanwhile, Holmes was as angry as I've ever seen him. The traitor inside the embassy was still at large and his client had been murdered before his eyes. That in particular made him livid.

> **(HOLMES** *and* **IRENE** *storm into the room.)*

HOLMES. Of course I blame myself! I should have seen it coming!

IRENE. Don't be ridiculous. Did you shoot him?

HOLMES. Oh don't try and –

IRENE. *Did you shoot him?*

HOLMES. No.

IRENE. Are you clairvoyant?

HOLMES. No. But I saw Moran this afternoon and I should have taken more precautions. I should have stopped him.

IRENE. Nonsense! You're a human being and you're wasting time. Go track down Moriarty.

HOLMES. *(Through gritted teeth.)* I'm trying to.

IRENE. Then do it. That's what you're good at. You do what you can in this world and the rest is fate. Otto was a very good man whose time had…

(A catch in her throat.)

like my sister, he…

(The same again.)

God dammit!

(She stamps her foot and weeps.)

WATSON. Meanwhile, the police had sent for our old friend, Inspector Lestrade of Scotland Yard. We'd had many encounters with this loyal specimen of the London police, and his first words to Holmes on arrival were typical of his kind, inquisitive nature.

*(**LESTRADE** appears. He's a grizzled policeman in an overcoat and bowler hat.)*

LESTRADE. Fer Christ's sake, 'Olmes, why didn't ya stop the bastard?

WATSON. *(To us.)* He had the voice and temperament of a meat grinder.

LESTRADE. I got me a dead king, an embassy full o' bookkeepers, and a howling mob o' reporters on the front steps.

HOLMES. What did the coroner say?

LESTRADE. Well let me see. It was quite complex. 'E says the man is DEAD. 'E was hit by a BULLET. Though I suppose with the curtains pulled, it was a lucky shot.

HOLMES. Not at all. He took aim before the curtain was pulled, and then, with the lights on, he could see our outlines in silhouette. Any word on Moran?

LESTRADE. None.

HOLMES. The weapon?

LESTRADE. No.

HOLMES. Where is Hilda?

LESTRADE. Who?

HOLMES. The housekeeper.

LESTRADE. Oh right.

(He checks his notes.)

I haven't met her yet. She sounds like a pain in the arse. She's in 'er room bein' hysterical. She says she was in love with the King. And my men found *this* in one of 'er drawers.

(He removes a large, wicked throwing knife from his evidence case.)

WATSON. Good God. It's a knife.

LESTRADE. Your doctor 'ere is very observant.

*(At which moment, **HILDA** and **IRENE** burst into the room in the middle of a violent argument.)*

HILDA. It vas your fault!

IRENE. That's ridiculous!

HILDA. If you did not sleep vith King, he vould *be* here!

LESTRADE. *(To* **HOLMES.***)* Is that Hilda?

HILDA. Yes.

LESTRADE. *HILDA, SHUT UP!!* Is this your knife?

HILDA. No.

LESTRADE. It was found in your drawers.

HILDA. I am vearing my drawers.

LESTRADE. Not those kind of drawers! Your cupboard
drawers!

HILDA. I have never seen it. I am not a spy.

HOLMES. We never said you're a spy.

HILDA. You think because I know about the *plans* I am spy.

HOLMES. Then you do know about the plans.

HILDA. Of course I know. The King told me everything.
I even knew about letters and *I hated them.*

HOLMES. So you read the letters.

HILDA. No, of course not.

HOLMES. Then how do you know that you didn't like
them?

HILDA. Because he wrote them to that *voman.*

HOLMES. Whom you hated.

HILDA. Yes.

HOLMES. And yet you posted Otto's letters to her.

HILDA. He asked me to.

HOLMES. And therefore you could have opened them,
read them and tampered with them.

HILDA. I did no such thing! Vhat are you sayink?!

HOLMES. I am saying that you took the plans out of the safe here at the embassy on behalf of Sebastian Moran who works for a man named Moriarty. I am saying that you took photographs of the plans and smuggled those photographs out of the embassy on microdots which you put on the King's letters. I am saying that you are a spy, a traitor and a killer –

HILDA. *You are liar! I am patriot! I took the plans for Bohemia!*

HOLMES. Except that Moriarty wanted to sell them to the highest bidder.

HILDA. *That is lie!*

HOLMES. Oh Hilda, please, you know better than that. At least you suspected, am I correct? Inspector Lestrade, I would like you to examine Hilda's room more extensively this time. Look for hiding places. The back of a cupboard. A false wall. You will be looking for photographic equipment as well as a machine that makes something very small called a microdot. While you search, you will put Miss Klebb under arrest and keep her locked up, as a thief, a spy and the killer of Otto von Ormstein.

HILDA. *That vas mistake! It vas she that should have died! Und now I vill kill her!*

> *(She picks up the knife and is about to throw it, when **IRENE** pulls a sword from a suit of armor and they have a short duel. At the end of it, **HILDA** manages to throw her knife at **IRENE** with deadly accuracy.)*

WATSON. *Look out!*

LESTRADE. *Christ!*

IRENE. *Ah!*

(*IRENE jumps back and the knife sails by her and lands with a thud in the wall behind her.*)

(*Beat as they all look at each other. Then* **HILDA** *bolts to the door.*)

Stop her!

(*Bang! The door slams and* **HILDA** *is gone.*)

(**HOLMES** *runs to the door but it's locked.*)

HOLMES. Damn it all! Watson! Revolver!

(*He shoots the door handle and pushes open the door.*)

(*But the hall is empty.*)

Scene Two: The Hall

(This dialogue goes rapidly:)

HOLMES. Where is she? She's gone. It's impossible.

IRENE. No it isn't. There's a hidden door. The place is filled with them. Wait, I remember. The light fixture.

(She pulls on the light fixture and a door made of paneling slides open and reveals a set of steps heading steeply downward into profound darkness.)

HOLMES. Steps?

IRENE. They lead to the river.

HOLMES. Which is how you visited Otto in secret.

IRENE. Yes, and this is no time for attitude. Let's go, let's go!

Scene Three: The Stairs under the Embassy

(They rush down the stairs, which are dark and winding and hewn from rock.)

IRENE. Whatever you do, don't close the door behind you because it gets too –

(Bang!)

dark.

(The stairs are now pitch black.)

HOLMES. Sorry.

IRENE. You're Sherlock Holmes. You're supposed to know these things. Ow!

HOLMES. Sorry.

IRENE. That was my heel.

HOLMES. It's pitch black.

(They go down and down, with the feeling of dankness and water around them. It's like descending into a dungeon, which is probably how the stairs and passage originated in the thirteenth century when the foundations of the house were built. We can see them now.)

IRENE. We have to be careful. It gets extremely narrow just about *Noooooo!*

*(****HOLMES**** has inadvertently tried to move past her – and they are now tightly wedged together between the walls. They're facing each other with their bodies pressed against each other, their faces about an inch apart.)*

Dammit! What are you *doing?*

HOLMES. *(Through his teeth.)* I did nothing.

IRENE. You tried to pass me.

HOLMES. I couldn't *see* you.

IRENE. Well now we're stuck.

HOLMES. Really. I hadn't noticed.

IRENE. Well what do we do?

HOLMES. On the count of three, take a deep breath. One, two –

> *(They gasp and try to make themselves thinner, and push their bodies this way and that, grunting and groaning – "ugh" "agh" – but it doesn't work. They remain stuck, still pressed together like a sandwich.)*

IRENE. Ugh!

HOLMES. If you ever tell Watson about this, I'll kill you. Ohhh... Rats.

IRENE. That is an understatement.

HOLMES. What is?

IRENE. Rats.

HOLMES. It's not an understatement. There are rats on our feet.

> *(Now we hear them. Really hear them.)*

IRENE. Oh, *God*. I *hate* rats. Let's try wiggling.

HOLMES. I beg your pardon.

IRENE. Wiggling. Like an exotic dancer. Don't you ever go to the clubs?

HOLMES. Don't be revolting.

> *(She starts to wiggle like an exotic dancer, trying to get free. He winces.)*

HOLMES. Is this really what they do in clubs?

IRENE. Yes of course.

HOLMES. Well God help them.

IRENE. You're supposed to enjoy it, even a little.

HOLMES. Do please tell me when that part begins so I can – ow!

(*Angrily, she pulls herself free.*)

IRENE. Oh, sorry. I hope I didn't offend your puritanical sensibilities –

HOLMES. Wait.

IRENE. Don't tell me to –

HOLMES. *Wait.* Just ahead. There's a light.

(*He whispers.*)

It's Hilda.

> (*The steps open out into a chamber, and we now see* **HILDA**, *sitting in despair, holding a bottle of liquor.*)

HILDA. (*Muttering to herself in Czech:*) Jak to mohu udělat? Nenávidím se. Kdybych mohl, zabiju ho...

> (*They nod to each other and creep forward, staying in the shadows, then they hide behind a rock.* **HOLMES** *pulls out Watson's gun, then springs forward, pointing the gun at* **HILDA**.)

HOLMES. *Stop!* Stay where you are!

HILDA. You. Puh. You vill never vin.

HOLMES. Put it down.

HILDA. Please. Kill me. It vill be mercy for me.

IRENE. Hilda –

HILDA. *You be qviet.* It vas you who vas meant to be shot today. Und I did it all for him.

HOLMES. For Moriarty, you mean?

HILDA. No, for *him.* For my *King.* Und Moriarty can kill me for it, I don't care.

(*Bang!*)

(*A gunshot explodes and* **HILDA** *freezes. Then out of the mist comes* **MORIARTY** *with a gun in his hand.*)

(*We now see* **MORIARTY** *for the first time. As Conan Doyle puts it: "He is extremely tall and thin, his forehead domes out in a white curve, and his two eyes are deeply sunken in his head. He is clean-shaven, pale, and ascetic-looking, retaining something of the professor in his features. His shoulders are rounded from much study, and his face protrudes forward, and is forever slowly oscillating from side to side in a curiously reptilian fashion."*)

(*Beat.*)

(*Then* **HILDA** *pats herself. She is not dead.*)

Mûj božde...

MORIARTY. That's right, Hilda. You are still alive. Do you have the letters?

HILDA. No. I...I had to leave them. They vere after me! *They vere chasing me!*

MORIARTY. You disappoint me, Hilda, but it's what I expected. You may go now. You did your best.

HILDA. You are letting me... –?

MORIARTY. Yes.

HILDA. I-I-I-I-I-

MORIARTY. *GO!*

> (**HILDA** *runs away as fast as she can.*)

> (**MORIARTY** *points his gun at her retreating back...but he does not shoot her. Instead he laughs and uncocks the gun.*)

> (*And now, for the first time,* **HOLMES** *and* **MORIARTY** *face each other, one on one. They both understand the importance of this moment.*)

Well, well, well. "Sherlock." My best student. How you have changed.

HOLMES. Villain. You betrayed me. You betrayed us all.

MORIARTY. No. I merely took advantage of your naïveté. You were such an innocent. And so trusting. Now look at you. The light is gone. You look haggard with experience. It's distressing.

HOLMES. I trusted you and you became pathetic.

> (*Bang!*)

> (*Crack!*)

> (**MORIARTY** *shoots the gun out of* **HOLMES**'s *hand, sending it flying.*)

MORIARTY. I am a very fine shot, you know, and could just as easily have put that bullet through your heart.

IRENE. Monster.

MORIARTY. Not at all, Miss Adler. I'm a very just man. I had no need to kill Hilda so I let her live. I have every reason in the world to kill you and Holmes, and so I will.

IRENE. And my sister?

MORIARTY. Oh that was unfortunate. She merely had to tell me where the letters were. When she wouldn't, I had to put her down like a dog.

IRENE. *Yahhhhhh!*

> (**IRENE** *cries out and springs at* **MORIARTY,** *but* **HOLMES** *stops her in time.)*

> *(She is so angry that he has to pinion her arms.)*

I'll kill you, I'll kill you! Let me go! Let me go!

HOLMES. *Stop! Stop it! He is baiting you!*

> (**IRENE** *stops struggling, but still has to be held and is panting hard.)*

MORIARTY. Well done, Mr. Holmes. Another step and I would have had to shoot her right here on the spot. *AND I WOULD HAVE DONE IT!*

> *(For an instant,* **MORIARTY** *loses control, and we see a snarling madman. Then he calms himself and turns to* **HOLMES.***)*

Now. "Sherlock." You have been pursuing me and making lists of my confederates. Oh yes. I know everything. But so far you have only a handful of them and I intend to keep it that way.

Don't forget, I taught you everything.

HOLMES. Latin and Greek.

MORIARTY. And how to *think*. And how to *dream!*

HOLMES. But not how to steal and cheat.

MORIARTY. Oh, please, you are such a child. I presume you found the microdots.

HOLMES. Yes of course. And they are now in the hands of the British Government. So I'm sorry to tell you, but you've lost a fortune.

MORIARTY. I already *have* a fortune!

HOLMES. And soon you won't. I'm taking it from you. And your plans. And your confederates. Everything's going. You will soon be alone on a naked scaffold, your hands tied behind your back, staring down at your own grave. Does that frighten you?

MORIARTY. Nothing frightens me, Holmes! Because you are nothing. You are a mote of dust. You cannot stand in my way, nor can anyone else. You are all too "high-minded." You say I'm evil. *But evil wins in the end! It cannot be stopped!* "Oh help the poor and helpless. Have a conscience. Have pity." My followers are loyal because I make them *rich*. They know what I'm doing, but they avert their eyes and pretend not to see. They should be in Parliament. And some of them are!

> *(He laughs.)*

Now any last words, "Sherlock"? If you tell me now, I'll have them engraved on your *tombstone*.

HOLMES. None. And you?

MORIARTY. *(Laughs.)* No, Mr. Holmes. I don't need them. Besides, anything I have to say has already crossed your mind.

HOLMES. Then all of my answers have crossed yours.

IRENE. *(A moan.)* No...

MORIARTY. Good-bye, "Sherlock."

> *(He raises his gun and points it at **HOLMES**.)*

HOLMES. Watson! Take him!

> *(**MORIARTY**'s eye flickers to the side to look for Watson, and in that instant, **HOLMES** springs and the two men wrestle furiously. **HOLMES** gets his hand on **MORIARTY**'s gun*

but can't manage to wrest it away. Their struggle is hair-raising, and each man cries out with effort and pain. During the struggle, the gun goes off.)

(Bang!)

*(**IRENE** ducks.)*

*(In the end, **MORIARTY** is the victor. He shoves **HOLMES** across the room, the gun still in his hand. He is furious and panting hard from the struggle.)*

MORIARTY. *Give me one reason I shouldn't shoot you right this instant?!*

HOLMES. *(Unperturbed.)* I'll give you three.

*(**HOLMES** holds out his hand and drops three bullets onto the ground – the ones he took from **MORIARTY**'s gun in the struggle.)*

Your bullets. It would have been six, but you fired three of them, one just now, one at me, and one at Hilda.

MORIARTY. *(Furious again.) ...CLOWN! CIPHER! THIS ISN'T OVER!*

HOLMES. But it will be soon.

*(**MORIARTY** cries in anger and stalks away.)*

IRENE. Stop him. *STOP HIM!*

*(She rushes towards **MORIARTY**, but **HOLMES** catches her and holds her back.)*

HOLMES. No, not now.

IRENE. *Let go of me! He's getting away!*

HOLMES. He's not. *He's not! Would you listen!*

(She stops struggling but is panting hard.)

HOLMES. I don't want only *him*. I want his people. I want all of them.

IRENE. But we'll never find him again!

HOLMES. We will, I promise. That is the point. We need to track him to his lair and find his confederates.

IRENE. But how?

TOBY. *(Offstage.) Roof! Roof!*

HOLMES. Because we have a new ally, and he's the best tracker in the business.

TOBY. *(Entering.) Roof, roof, roof, roof, roof, roof, roof!*

> **(TOBY** *the Bloodhound bounds in enthusiastically, dragging* **WATSON** *by the leash. He joyously woofs and snuffles throughout the scene.)*

> **(TOBY** *is played by one of the actors working a dog-sized puppet.)*

WATSON. Toby! Toby, calm down.

HOLMES. Miss Adler, my friend Toby the Hound.

TOBY. *Woof! Woof! Woof! Woof! Woof!*

> **(TOBY** *bounds onto* **IRENE,** *licks her face with affection and makes whimpering noises.)*

IRENE. Toby!

HOLMES. Toby, smell. The man's a villain. You need to find him.

> **(HOLMES** *is using Moriarty's white handkerchief, which he took in the struggle.)*

TOBY. *Whoof!*

(**TOBY** *smells the handkerchief, digging his nose deeply into it:*)

Snuffle, snuffle, snuffle, snuffle!

HOLMES. All right, Toby, find the villain.

TOBY. *ROOF!*

HOLMES. And keep it down.

TOBY. Woof...

WATSON. *(To us.)* And so we set forth, like Don Quixote, Sancho Panza and Dulcinea: the visionary, the shield-bearer, and the woman of light, all tilting at the same windmill, trying to save the world.

> *(They exit towards the light, then out of the tunnel and into Lambeth Wharf, a vast landscape of hulking ships and deep nighttime shadows.)*
>
> *(We hear the mournful horn of a distant vessel.)*
>
> *(Throughout the chase, **TOBY** frequently WOOFS! and snuffles enthusiastically.)*

Scene Four: Lambeth Wharf

(We're on a wharf that is largely deserted. The wind howls eerily, making us all the more aware of the danger surrounding them.)

WATSON. *(To us.)* A half hour later we emerged from the tunnel and found ourselves at Lambeth Wharf, a vast anchorage on the Thames where the cargo ships, black in the moonlight, were the size of mountains. It was deadly quiet, save for the wind and snatches of music from the distant taverns. As we approached the town, we saw that it was a dank warren of sinister and winding alleyways, and we knew that Moriarty was lurking nearby.

HOLMES. *(Whispering and urgent.)* Which way, boy? Can you pick up the scent?

> *(**TOBY** sniffs and pulls them this way and that, all around the wharf –)*

> *(Then **TOBY** lets out a loud WOOF and dives down a steep alley, taking the others with him.)*

WATSON. Wait! I hear something!

HOLMES. Careful!

IRENE. It's pitch black!

HOLMES. Wait! There's a light ahead!

WATSON. It's a window.

HOLMES. Stay down.

TOBY. Woof!

IRENE, HOLMES & WATSON. Shhh!

> *(The four friends crouch in front of the window and try to look inside without being seen.)*

*(They see **MORIARTY** inside the room, emptying the contents of drawers and folders into a suitcase.)*

IRENE. *There he is!*

WATSON. It must be his lair.

HOLMES. One of several, I believe. That's his trick. He keeps moving his headquarters, which is why I haven't found him till now.

WATSON. We should go inside and arrest him, red-handed, with the all the evidence.

HOLMES. Not yet. I want to see what he's up to.

(They watch him packing his papers; then they see him pick up his suitcase and head for the door.)

IRENE. Look out! He's coming!

TOBY. Woof!

*(They hurry to a corner of the street and watch, as **MORIARTY** comes out the door carrying his suitcase. He locks the door behind him and heads up the street, passing within only a few yards of our heroes. They wait to speak till he's far enough away so he can't hear them.)*

WATSON. *(Hissing.)* Do you think he saw us?

HOLMES. He showed no sign of it.

IRENE. Hold on. I have an idea. Stay here.

(She hurries away.)

WATSON. Wait! Miss Adler! Stop! He'll see you!

HOLMES. *(Trying to get to her.)* Miss Adler, for God's sake!

WATSON. *(Holding onto* **HOLMES**, *who is trying to get to* **IRENE**.*)* Stop! Holmes, stop! It's too late! He'll kill us all!

HOLMES. *And I don't care!* Goddam the woman! She is *impossible*! Despite what she thinks, she is *not* a law unto herself, she is *not* invincible, and she is going to get herself *killed! Damn, damn, damn the woman!*

> *(We now see* **IRENE** *transform herself. As an actress, she knows exactly what to do: she turns her jacket inside out, teases her hair, smears makeup across her face – and suddenly she looks like a tipsy woman of the streets, a sailor's moll. Then she stumbles down the avenue, singing at the top of her lungs – and bumps straight into* **MORIARTY**.*)*

IRENE. Whoa! Sorry Guv'nor. Watch yer step.

MORIARTY. *(Pushing her away.)* Get away from me! What are you doing?!

IRENE. What am oi doing? You be careful! I'm not that kinda girl, ya know.

MORIARTY. Don't you touch me!

IRENE. Sorry. I don't mean nuthin' by it. Don't be uppity.

MORIARTY. Guttersnipe!

IRENE. O'course, now that I'm seein' you up close like this, you're quite an attractive fellow. Perhaps we oughta get better acquainted.

> *(She tries to kiss him.)*

MORIARTY. *Stop it! Stop it!*

> *(She kisses him.)*

I said stop it!

(He grabs her by the throat and holds her up and peers at her face. Does he recognize her...?)

IRENE. *Not so rough, ya brute!*

(He shoves her roughly to the ground and she cries out with pain.)

AGH!

MORIARTY. If you want to live, stay away from me!

(He turns, revolted by her, and stalks away.)

*(***HOLMES***, ***WATSON***, and ***TOBY*** wait tensely as ***MORIARTY*** disappears, then they rush up to ***IRENE***.)*

WATSON. My dear, are you all right?

IRENE. I'm fine, I think.

HOLMES. Now what on earth did you do *that* for?

IRENE. I decided to listen for a change. We want all of them.

HOLMES. And therefore?

IRENE. I lifted his wallet. You said he kept a list of names with him.

*(She produces ***MORIARTY***'s wallet.)*

WATSON. You're a pickpocket?

IRENE. I learned it from a longshoreman at Marseilles.

*(***HOLMES*** takes the wallet and hurries to a lamppost for better light.)*

HOLMES. God in heaven.

WATSON. What is it?

HOLMES. *(With growing excitement.)* It's not a wallet at all. It's a memorandum book with a list of Moriarty's henchmen. Listen: Max Von Herder, Canterbury, meet 10th April. Birdy Edwards, Basingstoke, 12th April. Thomas Agnew. Peter Blau.

WATSON. What does it mean?

HOLMES. *Proof, Watson! It means we have proof after proof of past crimes, future crimes, a whole list of crimes!* And we know who to find and where to find them! *Well done, Miss Adler, well done, well done! Come! Toby! Loyal Hound!*

TOBY. *WHOOF!*

>(**HOLMES** *strides away,* **TOBY** *following with a crow of delight.)*

WATSON. *(To us.)* From that point on, events moved quickly. We took the list to Inspector Lestrade who worked like a dog to find the criminals.

ACTOR FIVE. "Like a dog?" Really?

TOBY. Rrrrrrr.

>*(Shakes head and exits with* **HOLMES**.*)*

WATSON. Sorry. The key to the operation was to move quickly and arrest all of Moriarty's associates before they could hide. The arrests began that very night, from Edinburgh to Port Isaac, one after another, and it was thrilling.

Meanwhile, we knew that Moriarty was feeling the pressure. Alas, he did more than just feel it, as it turned out. By morning, the attempts began on Holmes's and Miss Adler's lives.

The first was a two-horse van that tried to run them down near Welbeck Street and was gone in an instant.

(We hear the sound of the van and the neigh of the horses. We see it happen.)

(The van rattles by ferociously and they get out from in front of it just in time.)

HOLMES. Thank you.

IRENE. And to you.

WATSON. Then on Vere Street a statue came down from the roof and shattered to fragments at their feet.

IRENE. *AHHH!*

> *(**HOLMES** grabs **IRENE** by the shoulders and pulls her around him and into his arms to save her as the statue drops from the sky and shatters to pieces.)*
>
> *(CRASH!)*

I think that someone dislikes you lately.

WATSON. That was followed the next morning when they were openly attacked by a rough with a bludgeon.

> *(A **VILLAIN** in dirty clothes appears and attacks **HOLMES**. They struggle and we hear the shriek of a police whistle.)*

I have often admired my friend's courage, but never more so than now as he experienced what must have been an hourly sense of horror and dread. He refused to hide, however, and continued pursuing Moriarty's confederates, until, on the third day of the arrests, we returned to Baker Street, unsuspecting, but in for a shock.

Scene Five: 221B Baker Street

> (**HOLMES**, **WATSON**, *and* **IRENE** *are at the
> door of the flat.*)

IRENE. Wait, I hear something.

A VOICE INSIDE. *Mmmmph! Mmmmph!*

HOLMES. Quickly, the lights!

> (*They rush inside, turn on the lights and we
> see* **DAISY** *tied and gagged, struggling and
> crying out.*)

DAISY. *Mmmmph! Mmmmph!*

IRENE. *Daisy!*

HOLMES. *Untie her!*

WATSON. (*Removing the gag.*) You poor thing... what
happened?!

DAISY. (*Gasping, then crying out with terror.*) They –
they – they TOOK MRS. HUDSON!

IRENE. Mrs. Hudson?

DAISY. *It was awful! She was screamin' and cryin' and
they tied 'er up and she calls for me and I says "I'm 'ere!"
and she kept on screamin' and they took her with 'em!*

WATSON. Good God.

DAISY. *You gotta save her! Please! She was scared to death!*

IRENE. Who was it? Do you have any idea?

DAISY. I-I-I don't know, ma'am. There was four of 'em.
And the ringleader, he give me a note for Mr. Holmes.
'E says "you *give* it to 'im or I'll *track ya down and I'll –*"

HOLMES. Let me see it... "Stop the arrests or Mrs. Hudson
dies."

(**HOLMES** *is so furious he can barely speak.*)

Get me Lestrade.

WATSON. Holmes –

HOLMES. Lestrade. *Now!*

IRENE. I'll get him. I'll be right back.

(*She hurries out.* **DAISY** *is weeping.* **HOLMES** *kneels beside her and speaks quietly.*)

HOLMES. Daisy. Daisy, hold my hand...

WATSON. (*To us.*) Never in our many years of association have I ever seen my friend Sherlock Holmes so distraught. He comforted Daisy and even shared, I believe, if only for a moment, her confusion over the existence of evil in the human heart.

Then, within seconds, he embarked on the most remarkable investigation I have ever witnessed. He started out on his hands and knees, inspecting the floor and the rugs. Next he was up on a chair, surveying the sills and windows, catches, curtains, shades, he left nothing in the room unexamined. Smell, touch, taste, instinct, he was like a machine that was sorting information on little cards and filing them away in the hundreds of drawers inside his brain. When he was finished, he returned to Daisy.

HOLMES. Tell me every detail of what happened tonight.

DAISY. I-I-I can't remember –

HOLMES. Of course you can. Just relax and think. We'll do it together. Let's start with their shoes.

DAISY. Their shoes?

HOLMES. We'll work from the ground up.

(*She laughs through her tears.*)

DAISY. Well…lemme think… the-the ringleader, he 'ad beautiful shoes. With them kinda holes at the toe in a sort o' pattern.

HOLMES. Excellent.

DAISY. And there was mud on the left one! It was yellow, and 'e sort o' scraped it against that table, right there.

HOLMES. So he did.

DAISY. And the rest of 'em wore old ordinary shoes, like workmen, ya know.

HOLMES. Trousers? Coats? Hats?

(**DAISY** *smiles.*)

What are you smiling at?

DAISY. I just remembered: the number two fella, they called him Crowder, he lost his hat in the scuffle and he didn't notice and I saw me chance, so I kinda like rolled over on it and kept it under me. And sure enough, when they was ready to go, he looks around and can't find it, and the big fella says "Let's *go!*" and Crowder looks some more, then shrugs and leaves without it…and I got it here. I thought it was the kind o' clue you'd like.

HOLMES. Daisy. Well done.

(*He takes the hat and looks it over.*)

…Married. Left his wife. Works on the docks but as a foreman. Had a better job at one time. Lives alone. Brown hair, recently cut. Lime cream. Frequents…

(*He smells the hat.*)

he frequents a tavern… Of course he does, near the wharf where we saw the yellow mud. No gas at the tavern. Paraffin candles on the stairs. Not tallow, mark you, paraffin for effect. A gambling club. Of course, *of course!*

*(**LESTRADE** hurries in, with **IRENE**.)*

IRENE. We're here!

LESTRADE. *(Panting from the run.)* Mr. Ho–

(Pant pant.)

Mr. Holm–

(Pant pant.)

God 'elp me, I gotta spend less time at the pub. Mr. Holmes.

(He takes a breath.)

I heard about Mrs. Hudson from Miss Adler here and I suppose ya want me to go easy on them arrests for a while.

HOLMES. On the contrary, Inspector, I want you to double down on them. You're currently seizing two men a day?, then make it four, or six. I want Moriarty to feel it and be frightened by it. If he's going to kill Mrs. Hudson, he'll do it anyway. And if she's bait, he'll keep her alive for as long as possible.

LESTRADE. I quite agree. I'm on the job.

(He catches his breath and then jogs out the door.)

DAISY. Wait! I just remembered – one o' the men says one more thing, 'e says *"We'll get 'im at the falls."* That's all 'e says, but 'e says it twice. *"We'll get 'im at the falls."*

WATSON. What could it mean?

HOLMES. I'll find out. Daisy, we owe you a great deal. Take heart.

(He turns to go.)

IRENE. Where are you going?

HOLMES. A gambling club called the Rochester. It's down at the wharf. I'll wager it's Moriarty's current headquarters and that Mrs. Hudson is in the basement.

WATSON. We can only hope! Let's go.

HOLMES. I'm going alone.

WATSON. Oh no you're not. It's three or nothing.

IRENE. Thank you, Doctor.

HOLMES. ...Let's hurry then.

(On the street.)

Driver! The Rochester Gambling Club, and quickly!

CAB DRIVER. Righteeo! Snap!

WATSON. *(To us.)* We took a cab to the Rochester, and there in the basement was indeed Moriarty's current lair, but it was empty. There was no Mrs. Hudson, only files strewn around the floor, maps and notations on the wall, and it was obvious that the occupants had cleared out as quickly as possible. We hurried upstairs to question the club bartender.

Scene Six: The Rochester

(We hear the sounds of a bar and see a cocky
BARTENDER *cleaning a glass.)*

BARTENDER. "Moriarty"? Never 'eard of 'im.

HOLMES. Unpleasant fellow. Very much your kind.

BARTENDER. I beg your pardon!

HOLMES. Your name, sir.

BARTENDER. Thomas Fitzwilliam Prescott. Yours?

HOLMES. Sherlock Holmes.

(He pulls his gun and puts it under the
BARTENDER*'s nose.)*

And if you don't tell me instantly where Moriarty took
Mrs. Hudson, I'll blow your nose off.

BARTENDER. *(Terrified.)* Ahh! I-I 'eard them say Waterloo
Station. I swear it on me father's grave!

HOLMES. Your father is sitting in the corner drinking a
pint of stout. You have the same nose.

(He cocks the gun.)

Or had.

BARTENDER. *(Panicked.) All right, it was Paddington
Station! I swear to God!*

IRENE. Let's go! Quickly!

WATSON. *(To us.)* The very same cab was waiting for
us, and it took less than half an hour to arrive at
Paddington Station.

Scene Seven: Paddington Station

*("Clang! Clang!" We hear the sounds of the
station.)*

ANNOUNCER. *(Voiceover [pre-recorded].) Now departing
for Gravesend, Maidstone, Canterbury and Dover.
Last call.*

*(Thump, thump, thump, thump, the score
ratchets up.)*

HOLMES. This is the train. He's heading for the Channel,
I'd stake my life on it.

WATSON. Do you think he'll have Mrs. Hudson with him?
I mean, if she's still –...

HOLMES. We proceed on the assumption that she's alive.

WATSON. Of course, of course.

IRENE. What do we do now?

HOLMES. Stand very still. Use your eyes. They may not
have boarded yet.

(Thump, thump, thump, thump.)

*(The three of them stand together, their backs
to each other in a triangle. We hear the
sounds of the crowd swirling around them.
Then, suddenly:)*

IRENE. Oh my God, there he is! It's Moriarty! He's on the
train!

*(**IRENE** points at **MORIARTY**, who now sees
them. Next to **MORIARTY** on the train is **MRS.
HUDSON**, who's terrified.)*

MORIARTY. *Fools!*

(**MORIARTY** *pulls his gun and shoots at them,
and the bystanders start screaming and duck
for cover.)*

IRENE. The man's insane!

WATSON. And the train's pulling out!

IRENE. I see Mrs. Hudson! She's next to him!

HOLMES. Get on board, quickly! *Jump, for God's sake!*

WATSON. *I'm trying! I'm trying!*

IRENE. *It's too late!*

(*Whooooooo! Chugachugachugachugachuga.
The train pulls away.)*

HOLMES. *No! No!*

WATSON. Now what?

HOLMES. We take the next train straight for Calais. I think
I know where he's taking her.

IRENE. Where?

HOLMES. In the room at the tavern, this photograph was
pinned to the wall.

WATSON. "The Reichenbach Falls." Never heard of it.

HOLMES. It's in Switzerland. It's a waterfall and very deadly.

WATSON. "We'll get him at the falls."

(*Clang! Clang!)*

(*To us.)* We managed to stay on Moriarty's trail and,
as Holmes had predicted, it led us across the Channel,
then on to Paris.

From Paris the trail led from city to city – from Paris to
Reims, from Reims to Dijon, from Dijon to Zurich.

(*We see Europe passing by behind them.)*

WATSON. Towards the end, as we headed to the final stop, Holmes and I had some time alone; and in a very uncharacteristic exchange, he said to me:

HOLMES. *(Quietly.)* Watson, we are heading into what promises to be the final battle of this unexpected struggle. If I don't survive – and it is unlikely – please remind your readers that I could not have accomplished any of the feats that you have so generously attributed to me over all these years without having you at my side at every turn. We have been as one from the very beginning, and now, after all our hundreds of cases, I am not aware that we have ever used our powers upon the wrong side, and that is no small legacy of which to boast.

WATSON. Holmes…

HOLMES. Meanwhile, I ask that you and Miss Adler remain friends in my absence. I have formed a strange… attachment to her that I cannot explain, and I would be happy to know that you will be there whenever friendship is called upon.

WATSON. Of course, old man, but let's not be silly. I'm sure you're quite invincible, eh? Heh heh.

(To us.) I made a joke of it, but what he said pierced me to the heart because I had never before imagined a universe without Sherlock Holmes in it.

    (Beat.)

Soon thereafter, we arrived at the Falls.

Scene Eight: The Reichenbach Falls

(We now see and hear the fearsome Reichenbach Falls. Once more, we turn to Conan Doyle for a description: "The torrent, swollen by the melting snow, plunges into a tremendous abyss, from which the spray rolls up like the smoke from a burning house. The shaft into which the river hurls itself is an immense chasm, lined by glistening, coal-black rock, and narrowing into a creaming, boiling pit of incalculable depth which brims over and shoots the stream onward over its jagged lip. The long sweep of green water roaring for ever down, and the thick flickering curtain of spray hissing for ever upwards, turn a man giddy with their constant whirl and clamour.")

(The roar of the water is deafening as it plunges into a boiling pit, over a thousand feet below the ground.)

WATSON. *Good God! I've never seen anything like it before.*

IRENE. *In the States we have one called Niagara Falls and people go there on their honeymoons.*

HOLMES. *Why?*

IRENE. *I have no idea.*

WATSON. *(To us.)* We'd only been there a few minutes when a local boy came running up.

HANS. *Sir! Doctor Watson, sir! We met on the train. You are a medical doctor?*

WATSON. *Yes, I am.*

HANS. *Oh please come quickly. A woman who came off the train, she has had a heart attack! We need a doctor!*

WATSON. *Can she speak?*

HANS. *No sir, she is breathing hard and she is trying to speak but she is looking terrible. Herr Krauss, the station master, asked me to find you.*

WATSON. *Holmes?*

HOLMES. *You should go, of course. We'll wait right here.*

WATSON. *Right. I won't be long.*

HANS. *This way!*

> (**WATSON** *and* **HANS** *hurry off.*)

> (*There is a string tremolo in the score, denoting danger.*)

> (**HOLMES** *and* **IRENE** *are alone. The falls continue to roar behind them. They have to shout to be heard.*)

IRENE. *Was that a blind by Moriarty to get Dr. Watson out of the way?*

HOLMES. *Yes, of course.*

IRENE. *Is Moriarty watching us now?*

HOLMES. *Yes. Don't look around. Stay focused on me. Smile. Don't let him know we see him.*

IRENE. *That won't be hard because I can't see him.*

> (*They look at each other.* **HOLMES** *smiles at her joke.*)

Mr. Holmes, if anything happens, it's been an honor knowing you.

HOLMES. *That is kind of you to say, Miss Adler. For me, it has been more than an honor. It has been a joy. But nothing will happen if you do as I say.*

IRENE. *Are you always this sure of yourself?*

HOLMES. *Yes.*

IRENE. *Are you always right?*

HOLMES. *Yes.*

IRENE. *Did you say that just to make me feel better?*

HOLMES. *Yes.*

IRENE. *Well that's reassuring... Wait. I see something up there on the rocks behind you.*

HOLMES. *That's Mrs. Hudson. She's been tied and gagged.*

IRENE. *Let me go to her. I can circle around.*

HOLMES. *No. Don't. It's a trap.*

IRENE. *But I can do it, I'm sure.*

HOLMES. *DON'T!*

> (**IRENE** *takes a step backward to go around a rock, when* **MORIARTY** *jumps from behind it and grabs her by the neck.*)

IRENE. AGHH!

> (*He holds a gun to her head, and she freezes.*)

MORIARTY. *No one listens these days, do they, Mr. Holmes?*

HOLMES. *Let her go. Your argument is with me.*

MORIARTY. *So it is.*

> (*WHAM! He hits her violently on the side of the head and she drops to the ground, unconscious. He points the gun at* **HOLMES.**)

Well. Now it's just the two of us and I have the gun. I tried to warn you that it would end this way.

HOLMES. *As did I.*

MORIARTY. *Oh I see. You're going to defeat me now, is that it. Only this time the gun is loaded, I assure you.*

(He cocks the gun.)

You had no right to interfere in my business! It is MY BUSINESS!

HOLMES. *Someone has to stand up to evil. And as we do it, others will follow.*

MORIARTY. *That sounds to me like cheap sentiment.*

HOLMES. *It is the greater truth and will defeat you in the end.*

MORIARTY. *But is it worth dying for? Here? Now?*

HOLMES. *Absolutely.*

*(At this moment, behind **MORIARTY**, we see **IRENE** wake up. She opens her eyes and shakes herself. **HOLMES** sees it, but **MORIARTY** does not.)*

MORIARTY. *Excellent. In that case, what do you say we speed up the process.*

*(As he raises his gun, **IRENE** gets to her knee, into sprinting position.)*

HOLMES. *(To **IRENE**.) Don't be a fool, Miss Adler. I implore you. There are other ways.*

MORIARTY. *(Without looking round.) "Miss Adler?" Oh, please, Mr. Holmes. This is feeble at best.*

HOLMES. *(To **IRENE**.) You have to trust me. I have lived long enough.*

MORIARTY. *Oh really, Mr. Holmes. You're trying the same trick you used in London? It's insulting.*

HOLMES. *(To **IRENE**.) I would rather you live and continue the fight.*

MORIARTY. *I am not a fool, Mr. Holmes, and you're making me angry!*

> (**IRENE** *shoots from the ground with a roar and races across the rocks.* **MORIARTY** *turns and sees her – and she throws herself on* **MORIARTY** *with a cry of triumph –)*

IRENE. *AHHHHHHHHHHHHHHHHH!*

MORIARTY. *AHHHHHHHHHHHHHHHHH!*

> (*And they both fly over the edge of the falls and into the abyss.*)

HOLMES. *NOOOOOOOOOOOOOOOOOO! NO. NO. NOOOOOOOOOOOO!*

> (*The falls roar.*)
>
> (**IRENE** *is gone.*)
>
> (**HOLMES** *is in shock.*)
>
> (*He can't breathe.*)

...

> (*He staggers backward.*)
>
> (*Slowly –*)
>
> (*Slowly –*)
>
> (*The lights change.*)

...

> (*Then* **WATSON** *reappears in his own light.*)

WATSON. *(To us.)* I returned to the falls to find Holmes in a state of near-confusion. Together, we freed Mrs. Hudson; but even she, in her immense relief, could see the utter loss that Holmes was feeling. She tried to comfort him, but in the end, she wept for him. As did I.

Scene Nine: At the Hotel

WATSON. *(Continued.)* That night, back at the hotel, Holmes and I sat in our modest sitting room saying nothing for quite some time. Then he broke the silence and said, as though he felt the need to comfort not just himself, but me as well:

HOLMES. Life is infinitely stranger than anything which the mind of man could invent. If we could fly out that window, hover over the great cities, remove the roofs and peep in at the curious things which are going on, the strange coincidences, the planning for the future, the hopes and dreams of those inside, it would make all fiction seem stale by comparison. Everyone thinks that their lives will turn out well, and then the surprises arrive like little soldiers, marching over the hill and becoming visible, each one bearing its own little tragedy. I have lived my life in the harsh light of that reality, and in the end, I must accept what comes.

WATSON. We must.

(He stands.)

Good night, Holmes. I... I would like to say... I would like to say how much I admired...Miss Adler. And how I thought that you and she would make...at last... I was...

(He can't finish.)

HOLMES. That's quite all right. Good night, Watson.

*(**WATSON** doesn't want to leave, but he can't continue. He exits, closing the door behind him.)*

*(**HOLMES** is alone.)*

*(And for the first time in his life, **HOLMES** feels alone. It's an odd feeling. He tries to analyze it, but he can't. He feels utter sadness.)*

(Pause.)

(Pause.)

(We hear knock, knock, knock.)

Come in, Watson.

*(**IRENE** walks in. Her clothes are torn and soaked through, her hair is wet, her arms are raw, her face is bruised; and she looks utterly exhausted. Indeed, she looks exactly as you would expect someone to look who has thrown herself into a maelstrom and climbed out, rock by rock.)*

(She holds onto the door jamb so as not to fall over.)

(She is still panting.)

*(**HOLMES** stands. He's speechless.)*

(Time stands still.)

(His heart stops beating.)

(She falls to the ground, to her knees, in utter exhaustion.)

*(**HOLMES** drops to his knees opposite her.)*

(He tries to speak, and she puts her finger on his lips to quiet him.)

(He takes her in his arms and kisses her for dear life.)

(The lights fade.)

End of Play